Enid Blyton®

NEW

MALORY TOWERS

Written by Patrice Lawrence, Lucy Mangan, Narinder Dhami and Rebecca Westcott

HODDER CHILDREN'S BOOKS
First published in Great Britain in 2019 by Hodder & Stoughton

1 3 5 7 9 10 8 6 4 2

A CIP catalogue record for this book is available from the British Library.

ISBN 978 1 444 95100 4

Typeset in Caslon Twelve by Avon DataSet Ltd, Bidford-on-Avon, Warwickshire

Printed and bound in Great Britain by Clays Ltd, Elcograf S.p.A.

The paper and board used in this book are made from wood from respoinsible sources.

Hodder Children's Books
An imprint of Hachette Children's Group
Part of Hodder & Stoughton
Carmelite House
50 Victoria Embankment
London EC4Y 0DZ

An Hachette UK Company
www.hachette.co.uk
www.hachettechildrens.co.uk

Contents

A Bob and a Weave by Patrice Lawrence 1
Bookworms by Lucy Mangan 41
The Secret Princess by Narinder Dhami 77
The Show Must Go On by Rebecca Westcott 127

A Bob and a Weave

by Patrice Lawrence

Dada parked the car. 'Are you ready to go in, sweetheart?'

Marietta couldn't reply. It felt like the wind blowing off the sea was juggling her words into nonsense. She imagined the Mighty Miss Hummingbird from Dada's circus swooping down on the trapeze to pick the words back up again. Then maybe Marietta would be able to reply.

Dada put his arm round her. 'It's not for ever, Marietta. Please promise you'll give it a try.'

Marietta couldn't make a promise she wasn't sure she could keep. She opened the car door. 'Shall we go in?'

'I need you to promise, Marietta.' Dada raised his eyebrows. 'Please?'

She sighed. 'OK, Dada. I'll try.'

Marietta already knew that this was going to be hard. When the car had turned the corner and she'd seen Malory Towers perched on the cliff, she was supposed to be impressed. Dada said that the school had its own theatre, gardens and a swimming pool that was filled up by seawater. She was supposed to be impressed by that too. But how could she be? She'd seen the Eiffel Tower in Paris and Buckingham Palace in London.

Malory Towers looked like a castle, and that made her want to go there even less. Those towers at each of the four corners reminded her of the girls held captive in fairy tales, like Beauty in 'Beauty and the Beast' or Rapunzel, who had to let down her long hair for the witch to climb up. Marietta tweaked the car mirror to check her own hair. Her rows of neat plaits framed her face, just touching her shoulders.

Dad smiled. 'Your hair looks perfect.'

'Do you think it will stay like this?'

'Miss Potts has given you special permission to use the staff bathroom if you need to. But don't you think it's easier if you just tell everyone?'

She shook her head. Her plaits swung from side to side, as if they were saying no too. She already had her plan. She would keep herself to herself and just get on with it.

Dada said, 'Let's go. Miss Grayling's already waiting for us.'

Marietta knew that Miss Grayling was the headmistress. She had always imagined her as a cross-looking woman with deep frown marks and a mouth pressed into a tight line when it wasn't telling you off. The woman walking towards them did look like she could be strict, but she had eyes as blue as the jewels on the Mighty Miss Hummingbird's leotard. The sunlight on Miss Grayling's hair turned it from grey to bright silver.

Marietta was so busy studying the headmistress that at first she didn't notice the girl who'd come out with her. She was taller than Marietta with shoulder-length curly hair and a kind face. Marietta felt herself starting to warm towards her, but she had to be strong. She wasn't here to make friends. She didn't intend to stay any longer than she had to.

Miss Grayling offered her hand to Dada. They shook hands and she smiled at Marietta. 'I hope you had a good journey,' she said. 'Don't worry about your trunk. We'll arrange for it to be collected and taken up to the dorm.'

Marietta wanted to say that if Momma was here, she'd be able to lift out the trunk and carry it up by herself. Well, she used to be able to.

The girl was smiling too. She said, 'Hallo! I'm Darrell Rivers. Miss Grayling asked me to show you around.'

Dada nudged Marietta forward. 'Go on, sweetheart. I'll see you later.'

Marietta followed Darrell through the great doors into a big hall. There were doors along one side and a stairway curved up to the floor above.

'Don't worry if you get lost,' Darrell said. 'We all do at first. Most of the girls are pretty friendly, though, and they'll help you if you ask.'

Darrell was chatting away about the girls she'd be sharing a dormy with. One was called Alicia, who seemed to like playing tricks on people. Another one whose name Marietta didn't catch was really musical.

'And then there's Gwendoline Mary,' Darrell sighed. 'I won't tell you much about her. I'll leave you to make up your own mind. Anyway, here's where we have assembly, and you see those doors over there? We've got a gym and art rooms and even a lab! Do you like needlework?'

Marietta nodded. How many hours had she spent sewing sequins on to the performers' costumes?

'You and Emily should be friends then,' Darrell said. 'The only thing she likes is needlework. I'm not that good at it. I'm better at sport. I bet you can't wait to see the pool. It's amazing.'

Marietta looked at her feet. There was a little silence.

'That's all right. Not everyone enjoys swimming,' Darrell said. 'But there's tennis and lacrosse. I really hope I get in the team this year. Miss Remington says that I've got a good chance. What things do you like?'

'I don't know.' How could she say that she loved playing chase with Sid the Strongman's twin daughters between shows? Or how she used to love sneaking in to watch Momma in the ring?

'Malory Towers is a great place to find out what you

like.' Darrell headed across the hall. 'Were you at day school before?'

Marietta shook her head. That was a mistake. Now there were going to be more questions.

'Did you have a governess?' Darrell asked.

'Yes.' She wasn't going to tell Darrell that she'd learnt everything she knew from Professor Cerebrum, the astounding memory man.

'There are a few girls like you here,' Darrell said. 'This is the first time they've been in a school, but they get to like it. Well, they usually do. Come on. I'll show you the Court.'

Malory Towers really was like a castle. It was built in a square shape with the Court in the middle and the towers on each corner. In the middle of the Court was a sunken arena surrounded by grass and flowerbeds. Rows of stone seats rose up from the open space. If she closed her eyes, Marietta could imagine Ballet Belle, the horse acrobat, thundering around on the back of her beloved palomino, performing her impossible balancing tricks. Marietta had to hold her breath to keep a little sob from bubbling up.

'I suppose you don't want to see the swimming pool, do you?' Darrell sounded a little sad.

'No, thank you.'

'I'll take you back to Miss Grayling.'

It was hard saying goodbye to Dada. He promised

to write whenever he could and when he was too busy he'd ask some of the other performers to send her postcards.

'And when your momma's feeling strong of course she'll write to you too.'

Dada gave her a big hug and she watched him drive away until he was out of sight.

Marietta was staying in North Tower. The matron came to show her where to put her belongings. When Momma had to go into hospital to have Pearl, Marietta's baby sister, the matron there hadn't been very friendly. Dada had said that some people didn't like circus folk outside the circus. This matron looked different. She was wearing a flowery dress partly covered by a bright white starched apron. The apron ribbons only just met round her back, tied in a tiny bow. She seemed to sense Marietta's sadness.

'Lots of our girls are homesick at first,' Matron said. 'If you don't feel better after a few days, come and see me and I'll see what I can do.'

Marietta nodded and tried to smile. Matron really did seem to mean it, but she would probably change her mind when she found out that Marietta was from a circus family. Nobody needed to know that.

The dormitory was a long narrow room. Marietta counted the beds. There were ten of them. She'd never slept in a room so big before, or with so many other people. The little white curtains between the beds couldn't hide many secrets. She would have to be very careful. Her trunk was already waiting for her. She hung up her spare uniform and the new skirt that Dada had bought her. She checked her hair in the small mirror on the cabinet. She was worried that the wind had blown it about, but it still looked neat and tidy.

Marietta reached in to the bottom of her trunk and took out a parcel swathed in red fabric. She slowly unwrapped it. Dada said she shouldn't bring any of her circus clothes, but this wasn't really a costume. She held the red fabric to her face. Momma had used this material to make her favourite turban hat and she'd taught Marietta how to wrap it perfectly. Marietta slipped it under her pillow. Inside the parcel were Momma's boxing gloves. She cradled them in her hands. They were always heavier than she remembered them to be. She slipped her hand into one of the gloves and clenched. Momma would only ever trust Dada to lace them up for her. When Momma had entered the ring that last time Dada had been busy sorting out an argument by the ticket booth. It was Marietta who'd helped Momma into the gloves and pulled the laces tight.

She hid the gloves in her cabinet and sat down on her bed. She could see the sea through the dormy windows. She wished she was on a boat, sailing far away.

Not long after, a gong sounded. For a moment Marietta thought she was back at Randolph's Impossible Spectacular as it sounded just like the gong Sid the Strongman bashed when the show was about to start.

Darrell appeared at the entrance to the dormy. 'It's suppertime,' she said. 'I'll take you down.'

The dining-hall was on the ground floor of North Tower. Marietta noticed the girls looking at her curiously, especially a girl with long blonde hair who was staring so long and hard it was rude. Darrell introduced her to the girls on the table, but it was hard to remember everybody's name. Professor Cerebrum had taught her tricks to help her remember dates and names and places, but her brain was too tired now. The girls tried to be friendly to Marietta, but when she didn't say much they carried on talking to each other. Marietta didn't mind. She sipped her cocoa and let the conversations wash over her. She had to make sure that she made it through to lights out without any big mistakes.

A thin, sharp-faced girl nudged the tiny girl next to her. 'Look, they must be telling each other secrets.'

Matron and another mistress were talking quietly over by the door.

'That's Miss Potts,' Darrell explained to Marietta. 'Our house mistress.'

Ah, that must be the Miss Potts who'd given permission for Marietta to use the staff bathroom.

She was coming over. What if she told Marietta's secret? She was looking at Marietta! That's what she was going to do! She was going to make a big announcement about it! *No! Please, Miss Potts!* Marietta hunched over her plate and waited for it.

Miss Potts stopped by their table. 'You seem tired, Marietta. You must have had a long journey. Would you like to go up to bed now?'

'Yes, please.'

The table went quiet and she saw a couple of the girls glance at each other, as she pushed her plate away and made her wobbly legs stand up. She ran up the stairs, brushed her teeth and drew the curtains either side of the bed. She buried herself beneath the quilt. Soon she heard voices and laughter as the other girls trooped up. She didn't move.

'Ssssh.' Marietta recognised Darrell's voice. 'She's asleep.'

'She's a bit stuck up, isn't she?' That voice was sharper. She was the one who'd noticed Matron and Miss Potts talking. Alicia?

'I don't think so.' Marietta didn't recognise that voice. It was loud and a little bit whiny. 'I think you're just jealous that she had a governess.'

Marietta clamped her teeth together. Darrell had already told everybody that? Marietta should have stuck to her plan and not said anything to anyone. This proved that they'd only share her secrets.

'And I bet you're jealous of her hair,' the sharp voice said. 'It's much more interesting than yours, Gwendoline Mary.'

Marietta lay absolutely still. She couldn't even breathe. They might work out that she wasn't really sleeping and try to ask her more questions. She was saved, though. A voice called for all the girls to get into their beds. Soon there were just whispered 'goodnight's and then slow, regular breathing.

Marietta waited, then when she was sure everyone was asleep, she wriggled her head to free her hair. She gave her head a good scratch. That was better. She was used to getting up early. Hopefully tomorrow wouldn't be any different. She closed her eyes and imagined herself back in the bunk in her wagon. The shutter would be open and she'd lie there looking up at the stars.

Marietta was up before the wake-up bell. She checked her hair. Momma said that Marietta hardly moved at all in her sleep. That was going to be so helpful here. She made sure she was dressed and tidy while the other girls were still stirring. She took out her writing pad and a pen. Now would be a good time to write home.

'Hallo!' A sleepy face peered round the curtain. It was the girl with the long blonde hair. She was also the one with the whiny voice. Marietta remembered what Darrell had said about her. *Gwendoline Mary . . . I'll leave you to make up your own mind.* Marietta gave her the smallest of smiles, but Gwendoline still came and sat down next to her.

'I'm Gwendoline. You're the new girl, Marietta, aren't you?'

'Yes.'

'Some of the other girls are a bit sniffy about people like us, but I think having your own governess is better than stupid old school. Don't you?'

'I don't know.'

'Well, I'm telling you it is. I've had a governess *and* I've been to school. A governess is much better.' She glanced sideways along the dormitory. 'It's just the two of you so you don't have to put up with rude people.'

Marietta looked down at her pen and her blank paper, but Gwendoline was determined to carry on talking. She flicked back her blonde hair and leant towards Marietta.

'I'm supposed to brush my hair a hundred times before bed.' She tossed her head about. The sunlight made her hair shine. 'It usually looks even better than this. Do you have to take your plaits out every night?'

'No, I don't.'

Gwendoline looked disappointed. 'Oh. I thought we could brush our hair together.' She brightened. 'Maybe you could show me how to do my hair like yours. My governess can do big plaits, but not ones like this.'

Gwendoline's fingers darted forward. They were just a grasp away from a plait. Marietta couldn't jerk backwards in case Gwendoline was holding on to her hair. That would be a disaster. All she could do was give Gwendoline a little push. And it was a little push, but Gwendoline fell backwards as if she'd been struck by lightning. She howled, clutching her shoulder.

'You hurt me! You hurt me!'

'No, she didn't.' Alicia was standing there, toothbrush in her hand. 'That push wouldn't have knocked over a house of cards.'

'You didn't see!' Gwendoline shrieked. 'I'm telling Miss Potts.'

'And I'll tell Miss Potts that you're making a fuss over nothing,' Alicia said. 'Who do you think she'll believe?'

Gwendoline rubbed her shoulder and glared from Alicia to Marietta. She unhooked her towel, stuck her nose in the air and stalked off towards the wash basin.

Marietta gave Alicia a little smile and Alicia nodded back.

In some ways school was similar to the circus. You had to do certain tasks at certain times and do them as best you could. Normally Marietta would be getting up at first light to feed the horses or preparing to set up the tents and booths when they reached a new town or village. Everybody had to work together. Even the little children helped, sorting out nails and handing over hammers. When the last rope was tied and the last panel touched up with new paint, everyone cheered.

At Malory Towers Marietta had to remember what lessons she was going to, where they were and the work she had to prepare for them. It seemed that Professor Cerebrum hadn't been a bad tutor. Marietta was good on history dates and her mental calculations impressed the maths teacher, even if her algebra didn't. The mam'zelles praised her French accent but both agreed that she needed to work on her vocabulary. The needlework room was her favourite place. Her quick, neat work made her one of Miss Donnelly's favourites, alongside Emily. Marietta even asked the mistress to save scraps of material so she could make a quilt for Pearl.

Gym, though, was the hardest. She could only stand at the sides and watch as Alicia and the other girls shinned up the ropes and vaulted the horse. She'd love to show them how she could hang upside down on a rope or vault over the horse and somersault before she landed but she couldn't take the risk. She just had to make do with stretches and climbing the lower ladders.

The girls mostly left her alone. In the circus there

was always someone to chat to. Just before breakfast she'd sit by the strongman counting his press-ups while his little daughters perched on his back. Around lunchtime she'd try to find Miss Hummingbird or Flatfoot Freddie or one of his clown gang to catch up on any gossip about the other circuses. In the afternoon she'd be with Momma and Pearl and help make supper for later.

Dada had kept his promise and Marietta was receiving letters nearly every day. Miss Hummingbird had sketched out a design for a new costume and wanted Marietta's advice. Ballet Belle had sent a hoofprint from Dragon, her palomino. Dada's big scrawling handwriting told her that Flatfoot Freddie's sister was coming to stay. He was also worried that one of Dante's magical rabbits had stopped eating and nobody knew why. Momma sent lots of kisses and handprints from Pearl. Marietta stored all of these precious letters under the boxing gloves in her cabinet. She only read them once as they made her want to cry. She had never been alone like this before.

Three weeks after she started, Marietta was heading out across the Court when she was stopped by Miss Remington.

'Have you thought about trying out for the lacrosse team?'

Marietta almost laughed, but that would have been

very rude. She had never heard of lacrosse until she came to Malory Towers. The first time she'd picked up the lacrosse stick, the smell of the linseed oil had instantly taken her back to when she was younger and Dada's circus was much bigger. They used to keep elephants and Marietta would help rub oil into the giant creatures' skin to stop them from drying out. As she had held the stick she imagined her hands were as steady as a knife thrower's and as strong as Sid's. She'd been allowed to tie a band round her head to keep her plaits in place and – oh, it had been wonderful to run until she was breathless. She'd almost managed to score twice, but Marietta knew that the Malory Towers lacrosse team took itself very seriously. How could she ever be part of something like that?

'I've been watching you,' Miss Remington said. 'I think you've got great potential. Why don't you come to a practice after lessons later?'

'Oh, please do!' Darrell Rivers had coming puffing up to join them. 'You really might enjoy it.'

Marietta would enjoy it. That was the problem. She might end up getting too friendly with the other girls. Or, even worse, what if one of the other players raised her stick too high and it went too close to Marietta's head? Or if she ran too fast and the wind was too strong . . . She could already feel the ball of worry bouncing around her stomach.

'I'll think about it, Miss,' Marietta said.

Darrell seemed determined to make Marietta go, though. She caught Marietta after the maths lesson and almost marched her over to the changing rooms.

'I know what it's like to be new and not really know anyone,' Darrell said. 'The lacrosse girls are a good lot. Even if you don't make the team, it will be fun.'

The changing room was full of the girls' chatter. It was all about lacrosse. Maybe it wasn't too bad. Marietta relaxed. No one was interested in whether she'd had a governess or what her father did. They just wanted to know if she could play. Could she?

Darrell even walked her on to the field as if she thought that Marietta would turn and run away. The closer Marietta got, the less she wanted to run away. She couldn't remember a time when she hadn't been running or climbing or jumping. She could almost feel the energy buzzing through her body. It wasn't too windy today either, so she didn't have to worry about her hair.

Miss Remington made them all warm up first, then they worked together to practise throwing and catching the ball in the stick's net pocket. The teacher walked up and down watching them closely. She nodded with approval as Darrell swung her stick and Marietta neatly caught the ball – backwards and forwards. She and Marietta made a good team.

In the last twenty minutes Miss Remington set up a game. There was a little smile on her face as she placed Darrell and Marietta in opposing teams. The captain of Marietta's team, a tall third-former called Joy, gave them all a pep talk about strategy. Marietta found it hard to follow. All she knew was that it was her job to run around as much as possible and stop the other side scoring. All the other girls were so good that by the time she shot towards any dangerous attackers, another defender had got there first. It was still fun, though.

'Marietta! Look out!'

An attacker was running towards her. A defender appeared behind the attacker and raised her stick. Marietta saw the attacker's stick sweep into the air and the ball hurtle forward. Another stick swiped the ball into the pocket and raced towards goal. It was Darrell. She had a look on her face that meant she didn't intend to be stopped. Joy ran towards Darrell, her stick swinging down on Darrell's. Marietta heard the thwack, but Darrell still had the ball, cradling it side to side as she sped on.

Marietta was a defender. This was her task and she had to do it as well as she could. She barrelled towards Darrell, stick raised. Darrell saw her and started to dodge to the left round her. Marietta knew a false dodge when she saw one. She'd spent years watching the clowns practise their comedy fights. Marietta dodged right at the same time as Darrell did. She caught the surprised look on Darrell's face as Marietta checked her stick and the ball dropped out of the pocket. Before it reached the grass, Marietta scooped it into her pocket and, with all her strength, sent it soaring back towards her team's attackers. One pass, two passes and, yes! They scored!

As everyone cheered Miss Remington blew the whistle. 'Good work, girls.'

Darrell stayed by Marietta's side. 'I told you, you'd like it! Are you sure you've never played before?'

'No. Never.'

Darrell smiled at her. 'You're really good.'

Marietta let herself smile back. After all, a smile couldn't be too bad, could it?

'Marietta?' Miss Remington was running after them. 'I expected to be impressed by you and I was! You've got great stamina and a very keen eye. I'd like you to be on the team. It will be mainly subbing in at first, but I'm sure you'll earn a permanent place.'

Darrell grinned at Marietta. 'I told you!' Then to the teacher: 'What about me, Miss Remington?'

'Sorry, Darrell. You're not quite ready yet.'

Darrell dropped her stick. 'But Marietta's only just got here!'

'Darrell!' Miss Remington frowned down at her.

'That is not good sportsmanship! Pick up your stick, please!'

Darrell scooped up her lacrosse stick and stomped back towards the changing rooms.

'I'm sorry about that,' Miss Remington said. 'Darrell has her heart set on getting into the team. I'm sure she will eventually, but you just pipped her. Practices start properly after half-term.'

Marietta made her way back. Girls passed her, slapping her back, but she hoped that Darrell would be changed and gone by the time she reached the changing rooms.

Half-term arrived at last. Dada was driving down on Saturday to collect her. Malory Towers had organised a tea party for the families and there would be a concert by the best lower sixth musicians. Marietta didn't want to stay. She didn't want Dada to realise that now nobody was talking to her at all. She was also wary that people might stare at him. That often happened when they were outside the circus. Dada's face was tanned from all the time he spent outside, but Marietta's skin was still much darker than his, more like Momma's. When Dada tried to persuade Marietta to stay for the concert she reminded him that she didn't have long with the circus. They were heading up north to Blackpool in the middle of the week.

As they pulled out on to the road Dada said, 'Miss Potts is a bit worried that you haven't made any friends yet.'

Marietta stared ahead. She would not look behind for a last glance at the school. Now she was on her way home she was going to pretend Malory Towers didn't exist. That's if Dada would let her.

He said, 'Is that true, Marietta?'

'I don't need friends.'

'You do need friends your own age. They don't have to be instead of your friends at the circus. You can have as many friends as you want.'

It was all right for Dada. He didn't have to spend every minute of every day trying to keep secrets.

'And you need a good education, Marietta.'

'I had a good education with Professor Cerebrum.'

Dada laughed. 'He's taught you everything he can. That's one of the reasons why we enrolled you in school.'

'I don't need to learn anything else. I can just work with you.'

'Oh, Marietta!' Dada pulled to the side to let a dray horse and cart pass them going the opposite way. 'The world is changing. The circus won't be around for ever. It's so hard to get people to pay their money to see us when they could be giving it to a cinema.'

Dada started the car again. 'I'll make a deal with you.'

'A deal?'

'We'll give it until the second week after half-term. If you still hate Malory Towers then, I'll come and collect you. How does that sound?'

Marietta nodded. That sounded fair. Only two more weeks of school and she would be free.

The circus camp was pitched in a field next to a small forest. As soon as the car drew up, the door of a bright yellow wagon burst open and Momma came running out, followed by a short woman just about holding on to a struggling toddler. Momma grabbed Marietta and hugged her. Marietta closed her eyes and breathed in. How could she ever want to be anywhere else but with Momma? She eventually untangled herself from the hug and looked at Momma. Her skin was glowing and there was a smile around her eyes. It had been a long time since Momma had looked so well.

The short woman was Flatfoot Freddie's sister, Josie. She was relieved to hand Pearl to Marietta.

'She's a great little kid, but, phew!' She wiped her forehead.

For a second Pearl leant right back in Marietta's arms and squinted at her. Had her baby sister forgotten her? Suddenly Pearl bobbed forward and planted a wet kiss on Marietta's cheek.

'Matta!' she squealed. Marietta cuddled her little sister even tighter.

For three days it was like Marietta had never been away. She counted Sid the Strongman's press-ups in the morning. Even though his daughters, Star and Comet, had grown bigger in the last month, he could still manage a hundred. The Mighty Miss Hummingbird invited Marietta into her wagon for endless cups of tea. She heard how Flatfoot Freddie had bruised his toe when he'd fallen over his own floppy shoes and that Listo, Miss Hummingbird's most trusted catcher, had rheumatism in his fingers and might have to give up working on the trapeze. Twice a day Marietta watched Ballet Belle exercise Dragon and then helped to feed and groom him in the evenings. Most of the time, though, she spent with Momma and Pearl. Momma still got cross with herself for dropping things. Momma's voice was much easier to understand now, and even more importantly Momma smiled much more.

Pearl could stand up holding on to things, but she couldn't walk properly yet. However, she was the fastest crawler ever. If there was such a thing as a baby lacrosse stick, Pearl was quick enough to be part of Miss Remington's team. Josie Flatfoot seemed very happy to let someone else run after Pearl for a few days. On the last evening the circus threw a little bonfire party for Marietta. Ballet Belle played her guitar and Flatfoot Freddie and the other clowns put on a special slapstick performance for her. There were marshmallows to toast and Sid the Strongman made everyone pancakes in the giant frying pan he used for his breakfast.

Later that night, Marietta lay awake in the narrow bed in the wagon listening to the performers finish packing for the journey north tomorrow. Marietta was going in the opposite direction. For three days she'd been her real self, with no worries about Momma, her circus friends or her hair. In the morning it was back to her other life.

On the drive back Dada reminded her of her promise. It was just two weeks. Marietta could manage that and then she'd ask Dada to take her home.

The dormitory was quite empty. Most of the girls had gone home for the whole week. It was good to have no Gwendoline Mary sulking around and rubbing her shoulder every time she saw Marietta. Darrell was away too. Marietta didn't want to keep remembering the look of hurt on her face when Marietta had been offered the place in the lacrosse team. She wanted to tell Darrell that she could have it. Marietta didn't plan to be around for much longer.

The other girls started to arrive back on Sunday. Soon the dormy filled with the sound of chatter and trunks being unpacked. Marietta knew that the girls would be bursting to know what she'd been doing. If it looked like she was busy, they might not disturb her. She took her writing pad and pen out of her cabinet. She wanted to write to Momma anyway.

'Guess what I did?' Alicia's voice seemed to cut through the hubbub.

Some of the girls made suggestions, but Marietta kept her head down and carried on writing.

Dear Momma,
I'm back safely and am very happy that you are much better. I don't feel so scared any more.

'I went to the circus.'

Marietta's stomach pinged. Alicia was sitting on her bed, kicking off her shoes. Did she say she'd been to the circus?

'I've never been,' Mary-Lou said. 'Is it good?'

Marietta tried to listen without anyone noticing. She moved her pen a little bit, but not touching the paper.

'I was in the front row for the lion tricks,' Alicia said. 'That was good. The trainer even put her head in the lion's mouth. I could see all its sharp teeth and I really thought it was going to clamp them down round the trainer's neck.'

Some of the girls gasped. Mary-Lou looked like she would faint.

'The trapeze was good too,' Alicia said. 'I knew they were doing real acrobatics and not trying to trick you.'

Both her shoes were off and she was sitting on her bed with her legs drawn up. She rested her chin on her knees.

'The worst thing was the boxing. My brothers didn't want me to go in the booth with them, but I made them take me.'

Marietta felt like she'd swallowed one of the biscuits at suppertime whole. She had to keep her head down and not say anything.

'I don't think I'd like boxing,' Mary-Lou said. 'I don't want to watch men hitting each other.'

'It wasn't men.' Alicia's eyes twinkled. 'It was women.'

The girls gasped. Marietta realised that she'd dropped her pen and a little splash of ink was spreading across her letter.

'But they weren't really fighting,' Alicia said. 'It was all pretend. Me and my brothers booed.'

'That's rubbish! It's not pretend!' The words burst out of Marietta before she realised it.

'How do you know?' Alicia straightened her legs and eased herself to the edge of the bed. 'You weren't there.'

'I just . . . I just do.'

'How can you? You didn't see what I saw. It was all acting. They just pretended to bash each other. It was rubbish.'

Marietta tried to squeeze her lips together and stay silent. She dug her fingers into her mattress to make sure she couldn't move. It didn't work. The memories flashed back through her head.

She used to love watching Momma getting ready to fight, warming up, weaving and bobbing outside their wagon. Marietta would watch Dada wax his moustache until it was shiny and curled at the end. He'd put on his long red jacket and top hat and make his way over to the boxing booth. Sometimes there'd already be a crowd waiting before Dada even started calling the crowd to step up and have a go. Then the boxers would troop up. First it would be the men, Skinny Jimmy and Bullhead Basil. Dada would ask for challengers from the crowd. There were usually more than enough. Then, when the crowd thought that was it, the lady boxers would appear. Fast Fist Fifi and Knockout Nell.

There weren't always challengers for the lady boxers, so Momma and Fifi had to fight each other. It wasn't pretend. It was definitely real. Sometimes, though, Momma was challenged by a stranger. Marietta knew how Momma had a minute or so to try to work out how fit and old her opponent was before the match started. That wasn't so Momma didn't get hurt. It was so Momma didn't injure anyone else.

Marietta felt like she could remember every second of Momma's last fight. There had been a challenger, though no one knew that it was a real boxer from another circus. She'd just looked like an office girl. Marietta had helped Momma lace up her gloves then sneaked in to a front-row seat. The opponent had fumbled around, asking for someone to help her put on her gloves. The referee almost had to drag her off the ropes to touch gloves with Momma. The audience had shouted and laughed.

As soon as the referee stepped back, the laughter stopped. Momma's opponent took a big swing back and punched hard. It hit Momma's head. It seemed to take a very long time for Momma to fall. Marietta hadn't been able to move from her seat until that thump as Momma hit the boards. The Strongman had run in and lifted Momma out of the ring and taken her to her wagon. A doctor was sent for, but he'd said that they couldn't tell how badly Momma was hurt until she woke up. That's if she did wake up.

Marietta wouldn't move from Momma's bedside. She was the one who'd seen Momma's eyes flicker and then open. She'd tried to hug Momma, but Momma had screamed and pushed her away. Momma hadn't known who Marietta was. She couldn't remember who anyone was. Her memory came back after a few days, but the old Momma was gone. She had bad headaches and didn't want to leave her wagon. Her hands didn't always work the way they had before and sometimes she said her eyes went blurry. It was like her voice had gone blurry too as the words leaked into each other.

Now big-mouthed know-it-all Alicia was sitting there telling everyone that boxers like Momma were rubbish. What made it worse was that everyone believed her. Marietta swept her letter on to the bed and stood up.

'Come here and say that to me, Alicia.'

Alicia slid off her own bed and stood there, with her hand on her hips and a smirk on her face. 'Everyone knows it's true.'

Marietta's heart was banging so hard, she imagined the other girls must hear it. Someone, maybe it was Sally Hope, was saying that Marietta and Alicia should just shake hands and be friends.

Alicia stepped towards Marietta. 'You've only just got here, but you've stolen Darrell's place in the lacrosse team.'

'No,' Darrell said. 'That's not fair.'

Alicia ignored her. 'And now you're calling me a liar. Women can't be boxers. All they do is pose about and pretend.'

Marietta crouched down and took Momma's gloves out of the cabinet. The girls were so quiet Marietta could hear the rain hammering against the dormy windows. She offered the gloves to Alicia. 'Try to hit me.'

Alicia laughed. 'That's a stupid idea.'

'If you think women just pose, try to hit me. I'll dodge and then try to hit you back.'

Alicia's face was going red. A challenge had been thrown down to her. She didn't want to lose face in front of everyone here.

'Are you scared?' Marietta said.

Alicia plucked the gloves from Marietta's fingers. She held them to her nose and sniffed. She made a face.

'Yuck!' She dropped them on the floor.

Momma's gloves just lay there. Marietta looked at Alicia. She was smirking again. Marietta felt like Dragon had kicked her in the stomach. At the same time her head buzzed.

'Those were my momma's,' she said and lunged forward. For a second Marietta saw Alicia's shocked face before Alicia jumped out of the way. Marietta felt someone try to grab her. Another girl, maybe Sally, shouted for someone to fetch Matron or Miss Potts. Marietta didn't care. Alicia was trapped against her bed. She couldn't get away. Marietta charged. She saw Alicia put up her hands and then—

Alicia shrieked. Someone else screamed. Marietta halted, her face close to Alicia's. Alicia's eyes were wide and she was looking up past Marietta. Marietta touched her hair but there was no hair – and the air was cold across the top of her head. She turned to see where

Alicia was looking, but the heavy sickness in her stomach warned her. *No* – Marietta wasn't even sure if she'd said it out loud – *Please, not this.* Alicia was holding up her arm and staring at her fingers. Dangling from them was Marietta's hair. Alicia's hand flipped and the hair lifted in the air and looped down, landing on Gwendoline's lap. Gwendoline screamed and flipped the braids towards the window. They bounced against the pane, then out towards the night.

Marietta touched her scalp. She looked from one girl to the other. Gwendoline sniggered. Darrell wouldn't meet her eyes. Nor would Alicia, or even Mary-Lou. Marietta touched the bare skin and the soft patches of new hair. The sob inside her was too big. She couldn't stay. She pushed past the girls and ran.

'I knew that couldn't be her real hair.' Gwendoline ran her fingers through her own blonde strands.

'Shut up,' Alicia growled.

Darrell turned to her. 'Don't take it out on Gwendoline. You're the one who started it!'

'No, I didn't!'

You didn't have to go on about the boxing.'

Alicia's face was set into its stubborn expression. 'I didn't know, did I?'

'And you had to open your big mouth about the lacrosse team.'

'You haven't stopped complaining about it.'

Alicia was right. It wasn't Marietta's fault that she got picked instead of Darrell. Darrell should have tried harder to be happy for Marietta. Instead she'd stopped trying to be Marietta's friend at all. She picked up the boxing gloves and read the words stencilled on the cuffs.

'Knockout Nell. I suppose that must be Marietta's mother.'

She went over to Marietta's bed and placed the gloves gently next to the letter. Darrell shouldn't have looked, but she couldn't help seeing what Marietta had started to write.

'Her mother was ill,' Darrell said. 'I wonder if it's got anything to do with boxing?'

'That's what really upset her,' Sally Hope said. 'It was when Alicia said that women boxers are just pretending and don't really get hurt.'

All the girls looked at each other, except for Gwendoline who had taken out her brush and was swishing it through her hair.

'I didn't know,' Alicia said quietly.

'None of us really know anything about Marietta,' Sally Hope said.

'We know that she hasn't got any hair,' Gwendoline said, giggling.

Every girl shouted 'shut up' at Gwendoline at the same time.

Gwendoline sniffed and turned her back on them all.

'I'm going to find her,' Darrell said.

Alicia pulled a jumper out of her trunk. 'Me too.'

'No one's going anywhere.' Miss Potts was standing at the entrance to the dormy.

'But, Marietta . . .' Darrell looked at Alicia. 'We need to find her.'

'Matron caught up with her by the Court,' Miss Potts said. 'She's soaking wet and quite upset. She'll be staying in the san overnight.'

'Can we see her?' Alicia asked.

Miss Potts shook her head. 'She doesn't really want to see anyone at the moment. Maybe tomorrow. Finish unpacking, girls, and prepare for bed. I promised Marietta I would take this to her.'

Miss Potts went over to Marietta's bed, lifted up the pillow and drew out a length of bright red fabric. She folded it carefully and took it with her out of the dormy.

'We need to do something for Marietta,' Sally said. 'Something to show that we really do care about her.'

'We could ask Belinda to make a card,' Mary-Lou suggested. 'A really special one.'

'That's a good idea,' Darrell said. 'But then Belinda would be doing all the hard work. She wasn't the one who upset Marietta.' She and Alicia swapped an embarrassed look. 'We need to do something from us. Something really important so she knows that we mean it.'

'I've got an idea,' Alicia said. 'Emily, have you got your sewing box with you?'

Marietta lay back and closed her eyes. She could hear Matron bustling around the other patient in the san, a lower sixth girl suffering from flu. She let her fingers touch the soft fabric of Momma's turban that was spread out between her skin and the pillow. The events from earlier played back through her brain.

Marietta had charged at Alicia. It had felt right at the time, but now she could feel the embarrassment rising up through her neck and across her cheeks. How many times had Marietta heard people shouting comments at performers in the circus? Dada had always insisted that you ignore them. Even if it hurt you, you should never react. The last thing Mighty Miss Hummingbird needed was to be distracted when she was about to somersault through the air.

Marietta's brain flicked to the moment when Alicia realised she was holding Marietta's wig. It had always seemed like the worst thing in the world that anyone would find out, but now . . . she held a hand over her mouth to hold back a giggle. Alicia's face! And, even better, Gwendoline's!

She wished that she'd taken Dada's advice. If Marietta

had told them about her hair and Momma from the beginning, everything would have been better. Now nobody would ever want to be her friend again.

Marietta could hear footsteps coming towards her and stopping. A cool hand touched her forehead, then the footsteps bustled away again. Marietta lifted her head, wrapped the turban round it the way Momma had shown her and lay down again.

Next morning, Marietta woke up to see Darrell sitting on a chair by her bed.

'I hope you don't mind me visiting you,' Darrell said. 'I can go away if you want.'

Marietta felt for the turban. It had come loose in the night and was rumpled up across the pillow. She reached for it, but – well, it didn't matter now. Darrell had seen her as she really was.

Darrell said, 'Everyone wants you to know that we're really sorry.'

Marietta raised her eyebrows. 'Everyone?'

Darrell smiled. 'Everyone apart from Gwendoline, of course.'

'Emily's made this for you.' Darrell passed Marietta a bulging shiny purple drawstring bag.

Marietta loosened the strings. Momma's gloves were inside.

'We thought you'd want somewhere special to keep them,' Darrell said. 'And . . . I know I shouldn't have looked, but I couldn't help seeing your letter. We wondered if your mother is better now?'

Darrell expression was open and caring. That's why she was asking. It wasn't about gossip.

Marietta nodded. 'The last time Momma had a fight, she was knocked out. When she finally came round she couldn't recognise any of us or speak properly.'

Darrell's eyes filled with tears. 'I'm so sorry. That must have been horrible for you.'

'It was, for all of us. Even when she started to get better I couldn't stop thinking about it. That's when my hair starting falling out. I'd see it on my pillow in the morning. Then loads would come out when I brushed my hair at night.' She held up the turban. 'I started to wear this every day. Sid, our strongman, used to say I was keeping it warm for Momma, for when she came round again. Some people didn't think that she would, but I did. It was all I could think about, all the time.' How could she describe the feeling? It was like Ballet Belle and Dragon were thundering round and round her stomach every second of every day.

Darrell said, 'Was your mother in hospital?'

'No. We still had to travel around and perform or we wouldn't have any money. Doctors are expensive and Dada thinks that sometimes they'd charge us more because we're circus folk.'

Darrell looked furious. 'My father's a doctor. He wouldn't do that.'

If Darrell's father was anything like Darrell, Marietta believed that.

'I didn't tell Dada about my hair. He was worried about Momma and I didn't want to make it worse for him. Miss Hummingbird, our aerialist, was the one who noticed and told Dada. He asked one of the costume makers to make a special wig for me.'

'The one that Gwendoline threw out of the window.'

Marietta nodded. They looked at each other and started laughing.

Darrell said, 'Would you be able to come down to the dormy? I checked with Matron. She said she doesn't mind as long as you are happy with it. Alicia would like to say sorry properly.'

Did Marietta want to walk into the dormy with all the girls staring at her? 'I'm not sure.'

Darrell stood up and held out her hand. 'Please?'

Marietta picked up the turban and wrapped it tightly round her head. She would have to go back down some time, even if she was going home in two weeks. She pushed aside the quilt. 'OK.'

It was ten minutes until breakfast. The girls were dressed and ready. They all smiled and tried to hug Marietta. Well, all except Gwendoline, who sat on her bed looking like she'd just swallowed a bottle of vinegar. Alicia was missing too. The curtains round her bed were drawn. Marietta sighed. Perhaps Alicia hadn't forgiven her after all. Who could blame her?

The gong went for breakfast. Marietta expected the girls to race downstairs to the dining-hall. Instead everyone went quiet. The curtains round Alicia's bed were flung open. Out came Alicia. She was wearing her brown Malory Towers tunic and her orange belt and a towel draped round her hair, like she'd just washed it. She came towards Marietta, stopping just in front of her.

She said, 'I'm really sorry, Marietta. Sometimes I know I shouldn't say things, but when I start it's hard to stop. So I decided to show you how sorry I am.'

There was a big snort from Gwendoline's direction as Alicia's towel fell to the floor. Marietta gasped. Alicia's hair was gone. Well, most of it was; it was cut close to her scalp, with a few spiky tufts.

'I used Emily's scissors,' Alicia said. 'I did it myself as I didn't want any of the other girls to get into trouble.'

Alicia and Marietta looked at each other.

Marietta reached up and slowly unwrapped her turban. She let the red fabric flutter to the floor. 'Thank you,' she said.

Marietta moved back to the dormy after breakfast. Matron had tried to get in touch with Dada, but it was hard when the circus was on the road. Later that evening, Marietta sat in the common room, trying to write him a letter. On the sofa next to her Darrell was chatting about lacrosse. Team practice started tomorrow. Darrell said there was a girl in the lower sixth who liked to coach new girls. Darrell thought they could practise together. Across the room Emily had started a new piece of embroidery. It was a green and bright blue hummingbird for Marietta to hang at the bottom of her bed. Earlier, Alicia had wanted Marietta's advice about any tricks the circus conjuror might share so that she could try them out on her brother. Marietta needed to finish her letter, though.

Dear Dada,
I don't need to wear my wig any more, but I have this friend called Alicia who I think may need one soon . . .

Bookworms

by Lucy Mangan

After tea the girls ran off to get changed then headed outside. 'Come on, all of you!' yelled Darrell, skipping along the path. 'It's our last chance to swim before the weather gets chilly and Miss Grayling bans us on the grounds of hypothermia!' It was always a joy to bathe in the big hollowed-out rock pool down by the sea and Darrell loved the cool, refreshed feeling you got after a good swim. The others darted alongside her, eager to be the first to dive in and swim a whole length underwater. They pushed each other aside gleefully as they ran towards the diving boards of differing heights.

Gwendoline lingered unhappily behind, clutching her towel round her shoulders. Even at the height of summer she was never keen on bundling her golden hair, of which she was very proud, into a cap and she hated, absolutely hated, getting her face wet.

'Get a move on, Gwendoline,' said Alicia, turning and glaring at her. 'We don't have long.'

Darrell couldn't wait. She ran ahead and dived in gracefully from the highest board. Bliss! She resurfaced and watched Alicia and Gwendoline still bickering.

'The thing is, Alicia, I'm not sure that I want a swim today,' murmured Gwendoline, dipping a toe in the water and hastily removing it again. 'I'll just stand here and watch.'

'Oh, no you won't,' said Alicia lightly, giving her a little push. Gwendoline cried out as she fell into the pool. Darrell giggled and exchanged a look with Irene, who was trying to hide a smile. This sort of thing often happened with Gwendoline, the girls knew; it was almost as if she expected it now. Why couldn't she just pull herself together?

As Darrell swam back in a clean straight line Alicia gave her a wink and nodded towards Gwendoline who was still sniffing in outrage, gripping the edge of the pool. Darrell hesitated – it felt mean to torture her further – but Alicia's mischievous look was too tempting. She swam up behind the girl. 'Deep breath, Gwendoline!' she shouted, then ducked her under the water. Alicia shrieked in delight and Irene's laugh resonated from the other end of the pool.

Gwendoline bobbed back up, coughing and spluttering. Darrell's warning had come too late and she had tried to breathe in as she went under the hateful water. She was too shocked to speak. Then: 'DARRELL RIVERS, I've had enough, I tell you! I'm going straight to Miss Grayling!' she shrieked. She hauled herself out of the pool and stumbled off to find a mistress to complain to. Darrell sighed. What a nuisance! She felt a wave of guilt about Gwendoline's spluttering and now she was going to get into trouble too.

Darrell was already on thin ice for joining in with teasing Gwendoline last week (but really Gwendoline had deserved it, and she became increasingly annoying as term went on!) and on top of that a couple of mistresses had complained of Darrell's prep being rushed, which it had been because of extra lacrosse practice. Miss Parker had already told her that if she got into trouble again she'd have to miss the next match. At any rate it was exasperating beyond words if she was now to be punished for a simple dunking.

Once changed she sought refuge in the boot room, only to find that it was being cleaned, so she made her way to a little music room that nobody ever used. No luck! That too was out of bounds because the walls were being repainted. She strolled down the corridor, considering her options. She walked past the library out of habit, then stopped and turned. Of course! No one would think of looking for Darrell there. In the library she headed for the nearest bookshelf, relieved to see that nobody else seemed to be around.

Irritation crept up on her as she pulled a volume down off the shelf. How tiresome that her last swim of the year had been cut short! It was a bit much that Alicia had egged her on yet she was going to be the one blamed.

Alicia was a riot to be around but sometimes it cost Darrell dearly to be her friend. She flicked fiercely through the book, wondering if Gwendoline really was going to tell on her.

'Can I find you something you like better?' asked a dispassionate voice behind her.

Darrell jumped and turned round. An older girl bearing a LIBRARY MONITOR badge was staring sternly at the book in her hand. Darrell reddened as she realised she had been so worked up thinking about the unfairness of the afternoon that she had accidentally crumpled a page of *Mountain Flora and Fauna Volume 2* in her fist. And her still wet hair was dripping right on to the book and damaging the pages.

'Er, yes please!' said Darrell, closing the book and shoving it back on the shelf. 'This isn't – quite – the one I had in mind.' The library monitor winced, took the book down and dried the pages. Then she replaced the book, three spaces to the right of where Darrell had pushed it.

'It's important to keep the books in classification order,' she said gruffly. 'We use the Dewey Decimal System; anything else is anarchy.'

'I see,' said Darrell, even though she had no idea, in fact, what the monitor meant. 'Yes, you've got a jolly lot of books to keep track of, haven't you?' She'd never really spent much time in the library before and she looked around at the hundreds, no thousands, of neatly ordered volumes before her. The girl finished checking the spines on the shelf and gave her a suspicious look.

'You're Darrell Rivers, aren't you? Star of the lacrosse field?'

Darrell grinned. 'I suppose that's me, yes. What's your name?'

'Evelyn Hartley. Bringer of order out of chaos. So,' she said, gesturing at *Mountain Flora and Fauna Volume 2*, now back in its rightful place, 'would you like something on flora and fauna more generally? Or is it mountains you're interested in?' She raised a sceptical eyebrow.

Darrell hesitated before replying – was Evelyn mocking her? 'Oh, well, neither really,' she confessed sheepishly. 'I was just looking for a bit of peace and quiet, if you must know.'

For the first time Evelyn's face softened, just briefly, as if in understanding. Then she glanced around at the dozens of shelves. 'Well, what kind of book are you looking to borrow then? You may as well, now you're here, so long as you're prepared to return it on time. Something sporty? Funny? Adventurous?'

'I . . . yes, I like adventure,' said Darrell. She couldn't remember the last book she'd read, come to think of it, with all the extra practice she'd been putting in. Some of the other girls read with a torch after lights out, but she was usually asleep the second her head hit the pillow.

Evelyn led her to a different part of the room. 'These books are all fiction, my favourite section. Romantic stories, school stories, pony stories, adventure, fantasy – oh, why don't you give this one a try?' she said, her voice taking on a note of excitement. 'It's one of our newest books. I read it in two days, I simply couldn't stand to put it down.' She handed Darrell the book, stroking its cover. 'Try not to drip on this one, could you? If it's not too much trouble.'

Darrell held it away from her hair. It looked quite long. 'How did you manage that in two days, with lessons and everything? Are you terribly quick at reading?'

'Quite quick I suppose.' Evelyn looked around cautiously, before adding in a whisper, 'I pretended I had a horrid headache, they put me in the san and everything! I raced through a few pages under the covers every time Matron left the room.'

Darrell was impressed and shocked at the same time. She hadn't pegged Evelyn for a fibber. 'What's it about?' she asked. The title was rather strange: *The Lion, the Witch and the Wardrobe*. She couldn't think how the three things might be related.

Evelyn smiled, her eyes lighting up behind her glasses as if she'd been waiting for the question her whole life. 'There's a girl, Lucy – well, she's got a sister called Susan and brothers called Peter and Edmund, but she's the main one, very brave – and she goes through all these fur coats into a magical land of winter, but with no Christmas, see, where she meets loads of people, and a talking lion and Mr Tumnus the faun–' She broke off as she saw the bafflement crossing Darrell's face. 'Just give it a try for yourself. You can have it for two weeks.' Darrell nodded. 'Any longer and you'll be fined.' She went over to her desk and rattled a tin that was labelled New Books Fund. 'This is what the fines are used for, see, the money pays for new books to be added every term.'

Darrell thought the library seemed to have enough books as it was, then it struck her that perhaps the incredibly studious library monitor had read them all.

A week later, Darrell returned to the library. She was in a far jollier mood than her last visit and she tore down the aisles looking for Evelyn. She was surprised to stumble across Emily from her form sewing at one of the big tables in the middle of the room. 'Oh, Emily! What are you doing here?'

Emily looked up from her needlework. 'Hallo, Darrell! I'm often here. It's nice and quiet, which helps me concentrate on my sewing when things get noisy in the common room.' She looked down shyly. 'I just came from there.'

Darrell had been there too but hadn't noticed the softly-spoken Emily disappear. Alicia and Betty's mimicry of Mam'zelle had been rather over the top, she supposed, but such a scream – her sides still ached from laughing.

'Here's that book, Emily,' said Evelyn, appearing from behind a shelf. 'Oh, hallo, Darrell.'

'Hallo, Evelyn – *The Doll's House*?' Darrell said, looking at the book in her hand. 'I say, that looks a bit babyish!'

'I'll shelve that in my "uninformed opinions section",' said Evelyn. 'It's actually very far from babyish indeed. It's about love and loyalty in a family of dolls and I'd like to see you come up with something half as good. I chose it for Emily because it has a lovely chapter about the dolls' owners embroidering tiny chairs for them and making them clothes and I thought she might enjoy it.'

Gentle Emily flushed with pleasure. 'I will. Thank you, Evelyn.' She took the book and bowed her head, returning to her sewing.

Evelyn turned away and started organising a shelf. Darrell felt rather silly about her remark. Of course Evelyn wouldn't have suggested a baby's book, the older girl clearly knew what she was talking about. 'Here's my book back,' she said, tapping Evelyn on the back. 'Can I choose another? It was jolly good fun!'

Evelyn glanced at her. 'Which bits did you like then?' she asked, a challenging glint in her eyes.

Darrell didn't have to think for long; her answer came bursting out of her. 'When Lucy kept telling the others about Aslan the lion, that he was real, and they didn't believe her, and then finally when it matters the most he appears, and he's so marvellous and strong and noble! It was such a relief – I didn't want Lucy to have to go on without the others believing her.'

Evelyn nodded shrewdly. 'Told you it was good.'

'And Mr and Mrs Beaver were rather sweet,' added Darrell. 'I liked the bit when they all met Father Christmas. It made me long for the holidays.'

'The whole thing is magical; I've never read anything like it,' said Evelyn, taking off her glasses and staring into space. 'I've been longing to read it again. I love it so much. I want to make everyone read it! And then keep it for my children. And then they can keep it for theirs, and–'

'Perhaps,' interrupted Darrell impatiently. Why did the girl have to get carried away? She had to get to lacrosse. 'I don't have long, what've you got for me next? Perhaps something a bit more set in the real world this time.'

Evelyn concealed a triumphant smile. She was delighted that Darrell wanted a second book, but she wasn't the type to let it show. Besides, she thought it might put Darrell off if she appeared too eager.

'Well, this author is very popular,' she said, pointing

to some books by someone called Noel Streatfeild.

Darrell examined the covers. 'He seems to write an awful lot about shoes.'

Evelyn sighed. '*She*. And the books aren't really about shoes, that's just the titles. *Ballet Shoes* is a favourite of mine, about three very different sisters who go to a drama and dancing school. But look – here's *White Boots*. It's about a girl who's ill and has to take up ice-skating to strengthen her muscles and turns out to be an absolute whiz at it. As you're in the mood for Christmas, why don't you try that one?'

It sounded a bit drippy to Darrell but not as drippy as the ballet one, so she took it. 'Two weeks,' called Evelyn threateningly as she rushed off. 'Don't forget!'

'Are you coming for charades in the common room?' said Alicia to Darrell and Sally one day after lunch.

'Not me,' said Darrell, 'I'm off to the library. I need a new book, I've just finished the last one.' She'd been up every night reading *White Boots* with a torch. She'd admired the main character, Harriet, and the hard work and dedication she had put into becoming a champion skater, with her poor but warm-hearted family supporting her. Darrell thought she would mention the book to her younger sister, Felicity, next time she was home; she was sure to enjoy it too.

'You're always in the library these days,' complained

Alicia. 'Who would have thought *you'd* become a bookworm?'

'I'm not a bookworm,' insisted Darrell. She couldn't see herself becoming like the serious, bookish Evelyn, hiding away in the library and having herself sent to the san so she could read. 'But it seems a shame not to enjoy all those books now and again, and isn't it nice how they're all there, lined up and waiting to be read by us all!'

Sally nodded in agreement, but Alicia just shrugged. 'They can keep waiting as far as I'm concerned,' she said, walking off to find Betty. 'Deny it if you like, but you've changed, Darrell Rivers.'

'She doesn't mean it, Darrell,' said Mary-Lou softly, appearing beside her. 'She's just sore because you're chumming up to that Evelyn girl.'

'I don't mind a jot!' said Darrell cheerfully. 'Perhaps I have changed; people do sometimes.' She was used to Alicia and her sharp-tongued ways and she had learnt not to take her comments to heart. 'So what if I like reading?'

'I like it too,' said Sally, 'and it's far more pleasant reading books you choose yourself than when you're forced to read something dreary for lessons or prep.'

'Yes, and you're ever so busy with lacrosse, Darrell,' said Mary-Lou enthusiastically. 'I'm sure it's doing you the world of good to sit quietly and relax with a good book from time to time.' She gazed adoringly at her idol.

'Let's hope so!' said Darrell fondly. 'See you in class, both of you.'

One lunchtime a few days later, Darrell was on her way to the library once again. She had raced through *Tennis Shoes* and couldn't wait to discuss it with Evelyn. 'I'd like to know what you think of it,' Evelyn had said, 'as someone who actually likes tennis and knows the game well. It's odd – I hate tennis with a passion, but I enjoyed the story nonetheless. So maybe you'll like it even better.' It would be a jolly discussion; Darrell had enjoyed the story, but in her case it had made her long for tennis season when she could swing a racket again. Perhaps she could encourage Evelyn to give it a proper try one day too!

'Hi, Evelyn!' called Darrell as she arrived. She found the girl hovering at the desk where she filled out the library cards, white as a sheet.

'I say, what's on earth's the matter?' asked Darrell. 'You look awfully ill; shall I call Matron?'

Evelyn stared at her. 'Matron? No, no . . . but I need your help, Darrell. It's . . .' She pointed to the large reading table. 'On the Shakespeare. That big volume, the collected works. It's . . .' She couldn't finish her sentence.

'It's what?' asked Darrell, baffled. 'One of the sonnets didn't take your fancy?'

But it was no time for joking. Still speechless, Evelyn pointed again and Darrell walked over to the table. She gasped at what she saw. The old leather-bound volume, over a thousand pages long, was lying open on its spine, and inside the pages wriggled a pile of muddy earthworms.

A few more bookworms to join your club, read a handwritten card propped up against the book.

'It was there when I arrived this morning,' said Evelyn, keeping her distance. 'I can't imagine what it means, and who knows how on earth I'm meant to get rid of them. There must be hundreds of the things!'

Darrell sighed. She knew exactly who was behind this, although the handwriting had been disguised. She felt a bit annoyed that she couldn't talk about *Tennis Shoes* and she felt sorry for Evelyn who was still as pale as a ghost.

But it didn't seem right to name Alicia; after all they were friends and this was just one of her pranks, a fairly harmless one at that. 'I'll brush them off into this box,' she said, emptying one of paperclips on to the library desk, 'and take them outside.' She worked quickly, aware of Evelyn's discomfort. The truth was there were only ten or so worms, not hundreds, but the normally calm and unflappable girl was obviously terrified of the creepy-crawlies. Alicia couldn't have known this, though, as Darrell herself had only just discovered it, nor could she have known how much it would upset Evelyn to see a book damaged. Darrell wouldn't have understood that either a few weeks ago, but she was beginning to now, though she would probably never feel it quite as badly as Evelyn did.

'If we find the culprit, she'll be fined for damage to library property,' said Evelyn, her cheeks reddening with anger now that the worms were safely gone. 'What "club" do they mean anyway?'

'Who knows,' murmured Darrell evasively, brushing the final crumbs of dry mud off the pages. 'I don't think there's any proper damage done, lucky old Shakespeare. There you are, back to normal.' She shut the book carefully. 'Do you want to put this back in its proper place?'

Evelyn quickly shook her head. 'You do it, you're nearer.' She showed Darrell the gap in the shelf, still keeping her distance from the book. Darrell heaved it up, then went to put the poor worms outside, pretending she didn't notice Evelyn trying not to retch in disgust as she walked past with the offending box.

'You know, instead of fighting us, you could always join the club,' she whispered to Alicia later in history, a gleam in her eye. 'The more worms, the merrier.'

'What on earth are you talking about?' said Alicia.

Darrell raised an eyebrow. 'That trick you pulled on Evelyn this morning. I suppose you thought it was funny.'

'Who's Evelyn?' said Alicia innocently. 'I told you, I'm not interested in going to the library every five minutes like you are.'

Darrell laughed. 'So you *do* know she's the library monitor . . .'

Momentarily defeated, Alicia turned away and made a big show of putting her hand up and correctly answering a question about the Civil War.

Darrell returned to the library after tea. The worm incident had distracted her from borrowing another book and she wanted Evelyn's advice on what to read next. Emily was already there, sitting at her usual table.

'Is Evelyn around?' asked Darrell, briefly wondering what it was that Emily was always sewing.

'She's gone to find a mistress,' said Emily, an anxious look on her face. 'Somebody's vandalised a cookery book with bread and jam stuck into the pages.'

'Oh, no,' said Darrell, her heart sinking.

Emily nodded. 'It's true. Evelyn was awfully angry; I've never seen her so furious. She said it was no way to treat an innocent book.'

Darrell sighed. She'd seen Alicia asking for an extra

slice of bread at teatime, and now she knew why. She was baiting Darrell!

'It's simply ruined it,' piped up Emily again. 'The jam went everywhere, all over the cover and everything. Strawberry, I think it was. Evelyn said the culprit has to pay to have the book replaced, once they find out who it is.'

Once again Darrell bit her tongue. But later, in the dormy, she went up to Alicia when she was brushing her hair.

'I say, Alicia,' she said sharply, 'I know it's just a game to you, but the thing is Evelyn does find it awfully hard when the books are mucked about with.'

Alicia glanced at her, a glint of amusement in her eyes as she continued brushing. 'She wasn't hungry then?'

Darrell's frustration threatened to boil over. 'The book was completely ruined – how would you like it if someone completely spoilt something that belonged to you, someone you'd never even met before?' She gestured at Alicia's belongings on her bedside table.

Alicia scoffed. 'The books don't *belong* to Evelyn; they belong to the school.'

'I know,' said Darrell, struggling to explain. 'What I mean is that the books . . . they're like friends to her. It's worse for her than for you and me if something happens to them.'

Alicia guffawed, raising her voice and clutching

her chest in delight. 'Friends! THE BOOKS ARE EVELYN'S FRIENDS? Has the poor girl not got any others?' She looked around to see if anyone else was finding this as hilarious as she was.

I'm her friend, thought Darrell fiercely, but she didn't say anything more to Alicia. She hoped that now the point had been made and poor Evelyn had been humiliated, Alicia would tire of her silly games.

But two days later Emily ran to get Darrell from the dormy, saying Evelyn wanted her in the library. 'She's in the most terrible state, Darrell,' she said breathlessly. She darted off before explaining any more.

Darrell followed her immediately, only pausing when she caught Alicia and Betty exchange a look of pure delight. 'What have you done now?' she asked. They quickly adopted blank-faced expressions. 'Oh, don't tell me then, I'm sure I'll find out.'

'I do hope nothing's gone wrong with your new friend,' Betty said sweetly.

Darrell ignored her.

'I'll come with you, Darrell,' said Sally, and Darrell smiled at her gratefully. She feared that the prank would be even worse this time, so it would be useful to have her level-headed best friend around just in case.

As they arrived at the library a trio of first-formers walked out in fits of giggles. 'What's the big joke?'

asked Sally sternly.

'Hallo, Sally. Well, the books, they–' started one. 'The books–' She paused.

'Yes, the books,' said Darrell, urging them on. 'What about them?'

'Well, they're all back to front.'

'In the wrong order you mean?' said Darrell.

Evelyn would hate that; she liked having the books just so, in alphabetical order by author and then by title.

'Not quite . . . We can't explain; you have to see for yourself!' said the girl's friend. 'What an absolute scream!' They both dissolved into laughter.

Darrell and Sally exchanged alarmed glances, then marched into the library.

Evelyn was standing, arms crossed tightly, in the middle of the room. When she saw them she flung a desperate hand out, gesturing at the shelves. 'They did it overnight; it must have taken hours.'

Darrell stared disbelievingly. For a few moments she didn't understand what she was looking at. Slowly it dawned on her: every single book had been turned round so that its spine was hidden and only the white pages were visible. From floor to ceiling the shelves were a sea of white. A tiny part of her was almost impressed by the magnitude of the prank.

'Golly! Why would someone do such a thing?' asked Sally.

'They've put them all out of order too,' said Evelyn miserably. 'But that's not the worst thing. The worst thing is that they did it all so quickly and carelessly – I suppose they were afraid of getting caught – that dozens of the covers are torn and lots of books have been pushed inside each other, and their pages are all bent.' She shuddered with the horror of it.

Darrell could hear the pain in Evelyn's voice and felt rotten for her. The books did look an awful mess now she looked at them closely – this time, Alicia and Betty had gone too far. 'How awfully silly,' she snapped.

Evelyn breathed out slowly. 'I know I'm not the most popular girl in the school, but I didn't think I had any enemies either. But with the worms, the jam and then this – someone's got in it for me all right.' She scowled. 'I wish they wouldn't take it out on the books, though.'

'Did you say worms?' asked Sally with a frown. 'And jam?'

'I'll explain later,' Darrell told her. 'Evelyn, it's an awful shame. I can't stay now but I'll be back later to help you.' She felt terribly guilty about Alicia and Betty's handiwork; it was her they were targeting, not poor Evelyn. But she didn't know how to explain. She watched Evelyn gently taking down a couple of books with ruined covers and putting them in a pile with other damaged books to be mended.

'I'll help too,' said Sally.

'Thank you,' said Evelyn gratefully as she began sorting through another shelf. 'It's going to take an awfully long time if I have to do it all myself.' She stroked the cover of *Little Women* and seemed to talk to the book itself. 'Now I know how you felt, Jo, when Amy burnt your manuscript. Books are precious; it's horrible when people can't treat them properly.'

'Who's Amy?' said Sally, looking shocked. 'Did someone really burn a book? We should report it immediately.'

Evelyn smiled, amused despite herself. 'Jo and Amy aren't pupils; they're characters in this book, see. Jo March is one of the great heroines of American literature. Her little sister throws the book she's been writing on the fire and years of work go right up in flames,' she said dramatically.

'Why on earth does she do that?' asked Sally.

'It's revenge . . . Amy's punishing Jo. You'll have to read it if you want to find out why,' said Evelyn slyly. 'There's all sorts going on with the March sisters, you'll see! There are four of them.' Even at her lowest ebb she was still encouraging others to read, Darrell noticed. No wonder she had been made library monitor – she lived and breathed books! Sally looked unsure, but said the relentless Evelyn, 'You may as well borrow it. It'll be hard to find anything else in this chaos.'

* * *

'I really think it was beastly of you both,' said Darrell, seeking out Alicia and Betty later in the common room. 'I've just spent another hour helping poor Evelyn and we're nowhere near finished putting the books back. I'm exhausted.' She sat down heavily on a chair.

'Buck up! I thought you loved spending time in the library,' said Alicia with a grin. 'I don't blame you for getting bored, though; it is frightfully dull in there.'

'I wasn't bored!' snapped Darrell, standing up again so she could talk to Alicia face to face. 'But it isn't fair ganging up on Evelyn like that just because you're sore with me. She works so hard to keep everything in order. In the meantime nobody's going to be able to borrow a book! How will they find the one they're looking for, without being able to see the spines? I don't suppose you've thought about that, have you? You never do think of the consequences.'

'Yes, I suppose that will be a problem, borrowing the books . . . unless someone's looking for a good *mystery*,' Betty said wickedly, her dark eyes gleaming.

Alicia shrieked in delight at the joke, linking arms with her friend. 'You see, Darrell, it's all just sport! And, really, there's no need to queen it over us; you used to enjoy a good prank as much as the next person.'

Darrell felt her patience evaporate completely. 'I'm not queening it over you. I'm just explaining to you what a mess you've made.' They looked at her, baffled, so she continued. 'It may be sport to you, but it's becoming a real headache for other people, can't you see that?' She stared at them accusingly, her heart pounding as she remembered the look of devastation on Evelyn's face.

After a second of silence Alicia did a mock bow and encouraged Betty to do one too. 'We're sorry, Queen Darrell. Would you like us to kiss the royal feet?'

Why couldn't they ever accept any responsibility for their actions, thought Darrell, fuming. 'You're the silliest girls I've ever met,' she said reproachfully. 'And what's more I'm sick of the sight of you.'

'Well, we're sick of you too,' replied Alicia coolly. 'Now that you've forgotten how to have fun and prefer to spend your days chumming up to speccy Evelyn.'

'I haven't forgotten how to have fun!' Darrell shouted. 'I like the library, that's all; it's a good place to relax. Well, it was, before you decided to mess up the shelves, like the silly babies you are.'

Alicia rolled her eyes. 'Don't stew over it – you're getting duller by the minute. Old Darrell would be ashamed of you!' She and Betty sailed out of the room.

'It was just a bit of fun!' called Betty over her shoulder.

But Darrell did stew. She'd forgiven them the first two pranks, but enough was enough. Darrell had come to respect Evelyn and her quiet love of reading, and felt grateful for all the books she'd pressed into her hands. Each one had brought her a great deal of pleasure and it was so exciting knowing that there were hundreds more books and authors to discover – she would never run out! Thanks to Evelyn and the library Darrell had a new thing to look forward to every day, like she did with lacrosse. So the fact that those mean idiots had played such an irritating, heartless trick on her new friend – well, she wasn't about to stand by and let it go unpunished.

'We're getting our revenge,' Darrell announced to Evelyn as they put back the last row of books the next day. She had missed lacrosse practice to finish the work, and if there was one thing she hated with a passion it was missing practice. As a result her anger towards Alicia and Betty was at its peak and her mind filled with ways she could punish them.

'I don't want to make an enemy of them,' said Evelyn sharply. Darrell had explained who the culprits were and why they were targeting the library. 'All I ask for is a quiet life. That's why I spend so much time in here; books are *much* easier to be around than people.' Her face clouded over. 'Especially hateful pigs who like to meddle where they're not wanted. Why don't we just tell a mistress and let her come up with a punishment? Miss Parker was shocked when she saw the state of the library yesterday; she'll make them pay. Then that will be an end to it.'

Darrell passed Evelyn another book before replying. Alicia and Betty would know it was her who'd told tales, if they got in trouble, and then there would be hell to pay. Better to handle this on her own, and besides it would be more satisfying to exact the perfect revenge herself. She tried to explain to Evelyn. 'Don't worry, I'll leave you out of it,' she promised. 'I shan't even tell you what I've got in mind, if you prefer.'

'Please don't,' said Evelyn briskly, sliding a book into its place. She straightened up and adjusted her badge. 'I'm too old to bother with these silly games.'

Secretly, though, the girl was touched that loyal Darrell was taking her side, as honest and steadfast as Aslan the lion. Evelyn had always been quiet and bookish and was used to people ignoring or overlooking her. So when someone chose to stick by her it came as a pleasant surprise. In this case it almost made up for the horrid shelf prank that would haunt her dreams for years to come, she was sure of it. She still hadn't got over the shock of walking into the library and seeing the miles and miles of white emptiness stretching out before her, instead of the hundreds of dear, familiar spines that usually looked at her.

'I'm going to need your help, both of you,' said Darrell firmly to Mary-Lou and Emily, cornering them later that day after gym. 'You've seen what's been happening in the library – we need to get our own back. Alicia thinks I've become dull and forgotten the fun of a prank, but I'll show her what I can do!'

'I'm sure you'll come up with something splendid,' said Mary-Lou at once. 'And if you need a helping hand with it, I'm here!'

Emily felt a bit scared, on the other hand. She never got involved with any tricks and she especially didn't like loud noises – could they be part of Darrell's plan? Or something messy like stink bombs? Still, the library had been a sanctuary for her since she'd started at Malory Towers, and Evelyn had been kind, so now was the time to be brave. She swallowed her nerves. 'Me too,' she said softly. 'I'll do anything, anything at all.'

'Jolly good,' said Darrell. She had chosen not to involve Sally because she might try to talk her out of what she was planning. Like Evelyn, Sally preferred to keep her distance from schoolgirl pranks. 'What I'd like you to do . . .' she began, a smile creeping over her face.

'I say, I didn't know worms could be poisonous,' whispered Emily, her nose in a nature book.

'Louder,' murmured Darrell, looking around. There were about a dozen girls sitting around in the common room, most of them listening to Alicia's one-woman show. This time she was mimicking Mr Young the music teacher, twiddling an imaginary moustache and twisting round to see the pink chalk on the back of his suit – the result of a prank the previous term. The laughter grew louder and louder.

'Poisonous?' enquired Mary-Lou, raising her eyebrows as high as they would go. Nobody took any notice.

'Yes, poisonous,' said Emily, clearing her throat anxiously. 'Very, very poisonous.'

Darrell who was pretending to be absorbed in her novel on the other side of the room, mouthed 'louder' again.

Emily stood up and flicked through a few pages. 'Oh, dear me, yes, even some types of earthworm can be toxic it says here,' she said more loudly, and Darrell gave her an encouraging smile. Emily's little voice got stronger. 'That must be why gardeners always wear gloves.'

Betty glanced over. 'What's that you're saying, about worms?' she asked, breaking away from the others.

Emily went quiet, panicked now that the trick was starting to work, 'Oh, nothing,' jumped in Mary-Lou. 'It's just this book Evelyn recommended to us, about insects and creepy-crawlies. Lots of new information from scientists, things they've only just found out about. I'm sure you'd find it terribly boring.'

'Sounds dull,' agreed Betty. But Darrell noted a flicker of concern in the dark-haired girl's face before she returned to laughing with the others.

'Here's a list of the symptoms,' whispered Emily, trying to pluck up her courage again. Darrell sighed. This was the last time she would involve her in a trick; the poor girl was too timid for words!

'WHAT ARE THE SYMPTOMS?' bellowed Mary-Lou, noticing Darrell's frustration.

At this half the group turned round, including Alicia, and Emily's face glowed red with all the attention.

'It depends,' she managed. 'It sometimes starts with a mild rash in anyone who's touched the worms.' She turned a page and followed the text closely with her finger. 'Then it becomes a sore throat.' Darrell had noticed lozenges on Betty's desk the previous day.

'Talking of rashes, I woke up this morning with these three spots on my hand,' murmured Alicia, glancing down at the little red dots. 'I'd quite forgotten they were there. I've never had a rash before.'

'How serious does it get, Emily?' asked Mary-Lou, sticking to the script.

'It creeps up on you slowly, just days after you've touched the worms,' said Emily, reading from the book, and turning another page for good measure. 'If you're unlucky enough to have touched this particular species. After the rash and sore throat, the poison starts working its way around your whole body. Soon you become faint and breathless and before you know it you're in a coma.' She looked up, her little face full of concern. 'Hi, Betty, Alicia – did you wash your hands after pulling that silly bookworm trick in the library?'

Betty and Alicia looked at each other and said nothing, standing very still.

'It's very unlikely it would be this particular species, of course,' said Mary-Lou, 'and you both seem on perfectly good form so I doubt we need to worry. Did you *both* touch the worms?' she asked casually.

'Yes, we dug them out together, but I didn't wash my hands, and I did have the sorest throat all day yesterday!' exploded Betty.

Alicia went pale as she remembered hastily brushing the dirt from her hands. She hadn't had time to wash her hands either as she had fled from the library. 'My throat's feeling a bit scratchy right now. And just look at my hand.' She didn't know where the faint dots had come from, but this was certainly one explanation. Then she thought of something. 'What about you, Darrell? Didn't you help Evelyn clear the worms away?'

Darrell nodded, still semi-engrossed in her book. 'I did, but I washed my hands as it was right before lunch. Evelyn didn't touch them.'

'Oh, dear,' whispered Emily, examining Alicia's hand. 'Perhaps you should both go and see Matron.'

'Just to be on the safe side,' added Mary-Lou.

'You *have* gone very white, Alicia,' said Betty, trembling. 'Do you feel faint and breathless?'

Alicia patted her chest. 'I do feel breathless, come to think of it.' Her heart was racing. The other girls started talking in a panic and began to bring glasses of water to Alicia and Betty, fanning them with their hands, inspecting Alicia's rash.

'Maybe we should stay away from them,' Gwendoline said anxiously. 'It's probably catching.' She glanced at her hand, looking for rashes. All the girls moved quickly to the other side of the room, near Darrell, Mary-Lou and Emily, leaving Alice and Betty marooned.

Emily shut the book. 'I'm sure there's no need for panic,' she said softly. 'I didn't mean to worry you. It says that it's very rare for people to have an extreme reaction. I shouldn't have mentioned the coma, that only happens to one in five people.' She noticed Darrell egging her on out of the corner of her eye. 'Alicia and Betty just had a bit of fun with the worms, and now they've probably caught a minor cold, that's all. It's just a coincidence.'

Alicia and Betty exchanged terrified glances, then ran out of the room together, wailing as one.

There was a deadly silence in the common room. Then Sally glanced at Emily uncertainly. 'May I see the book?'

'Good idea,' said Darrell, erupting into peals of laughter. 'Oh, Emily, Mary-Lou, I do hope you've made proper sense of it.' Mary-Lou and then even timid

Emily joined in, laughing their heads off, and as the others gathered round Sally to read they slowly joined in with the laughter too, realising that the biggest trick of the week had just been played in plain view, and that the biggest prankster of them all had fallen for it!

'Then she went as pale as a sheet and declared "I do feel breathless!"' finished Darrell with glee as she returned the insect book to Evelyn. 'They were completely terrified, the pair of them, and ended up running off to Matron in a mad panic.'

Evelyn shook her head. 'Silly idiots,' she said drily. 'Perhaps if they weren't so scared of having their nose in a book they'd have a bit more common sense.'

'We *did* play it extremely well,' said Darrell. 'Especially timid little Emily! As well as reading out loud she was the one who drew the dots on Alicia's hand in the middle of the night. I wouldn't have had the nerve! The whole thing went so smoothly that everyone else believed us too.'

'So what happened next?' asked Evelyn, fascinated and delighted despite herself. 'Did they talk to Matron?'

'Oh golly, yes,' said Darrell. 'Mary-Lou ran down after them and says they caused a right old scene, insisting that their parents be called at once, that they were deathly ill! Then Matron took one look at Alicia's spots and washed them off with water, which is when they began to realise they'd been had. They still weren't sure, though, and when they came back up to the common room Alicia insisted on reading this book from cover to cover to check that Emily and Mary-Lou had definitely been making it up.'

Evelyn smiled. 'In that case it's all been worthwhile. Alicia has read a book! I do hope I'll see her in here in the coming weeks, and that Betty too – plenty more books for them to discover.'

Darrell burst out laughing. 'I wouldn't count on it if I were you.'

Just then she was proved wrong as a solemn-faced Alicia appeared at Evelyn's desk, the quick-witted girl for once seeming lost for words.

'How are you feeling, Alicia?' said Darrell mischievously.

Evelyn looked the girl up and down; it was the first time she'd set eyes on the perpetrator of the crimes against her beloved books. 'I was just telling Evelyn here about your unfortunate reaction to the worms. I do hope the rash is clearing up.'

'Yes, all right, Darrell, very funny,' snapped Alicia. She looked around. The shelves were back in tip-top condition. 'Looks nice in here,' she offered grudgingly to Evelyn.

'Thanks to all of our hard work,' said Evelyn coldly

after a pause. 'And no thanks to you and your friend – Betty, is it?'

'Yes,' said Alicia sheepishly. 'But mainly me. Look, I've come here to tell you I'm sorry about all of that.'

Darrell was about to make a cutting remark when she noticed the curious expression on Evelyn's face and realised she too was interested to hear what Alicia would say.

'I took it too far, I know I did,' the girl continued guiltily. 'But I suppose I was just angry about Darrell spending all of her time here.'

'But why?' asked Darrell, mystified. 'What could it possibly matter to you?'

'At first it didn't,' said Alicia with a sigh. 'It was just a bit of fun. But the more you told me off, and the more you spent time here, I felt sillier and sillier about everything. Which made me do even sillier things, I suppose,' she huffed, fiddling with the new books tin.

Darrell raised her eyebrows. 'I was just sticking up for Evelyn. I didn't think you cared a jot.'

'Well, I thought I'd lost you to some snooty secret librarians' club,' said Alicia. She looked down at her shoes. 'And that I wasn't clever enough to be a member.'

'Hardly!' said Darrell. 'Nothing's changed. I've just read a few books, that's all. And you're the cleverest girl in our form, you know that!'

'There's nothing secret about the library,' added Evelyn earnestly. 'Everyone's welcome!' Her tone changed. 'So long as they're prepared to respect the books, that is.'

Alicia's face relaxed a bit. 'Well, I can see I took it over the top, so I'm sorry for being an idiot, Evelyn, and making a mess of your library.' She glanced at Darrell. 'Although I did think the bookworm thing was quite funny!'

Darrell grinned. 'It was, although poor Evelyn can't bear the things. You've always been clever and full of fun, that's why we love you!'

Alicia's face lit up. 'I say, Darrell, now that we've all made friends again, why don't you come with me for a chat? I've got this idea brewing about how to catch out Miss Parker in the next class. She's been most frightfully boring this term, don't you think?'

Darrell was tempted to hear what her friend had in mind. But there was something she'd promised to do first. 'Tell me later,' she told Alicia. 'Evelyn was about to go through the new books list with me, to decide which books to buy with the library fines from last term.' She was rewarded with a grateful grin from Evelyn.

Alicia nodded. 'If you want something for the lower forms, my favourite book as a girl was *Mary Poppins*. My grandparents always read it to me when we visited them; it was nice,' she said airily. She dug her hand into her pocket, dropped a coin in the tin, and walked off to find Betty.

Darrell watched her go. 'You can go with her if you want. I don't mind,' said Evelyn.

'No, I'd like to help you choose the new books,' said Darrell quickly. 'I can find out about the prank later.'

'If you're sure,' said Evelyn, shrugging.

'Of course I am!' said Darrell, looking around the peaceful, neatly ordered room. 'It's so lovely and calm here, and I've had quite enough excitement for the time being. People like Alicia think you have to choose between reading and livelier things, but I say it's nice to do both!'

Evelyn nodded, adjusting her glasses. 'In that case – let's get to work,' she said briskly.

The Secret Princess

by Narinder Dhami

'Who's *that*?' Darrell Rivers nudged her best friend Sally Hope as they followed the rest of the chattering third-formers into the dining-hall. Darrell had immediately noticed a girl she'd never seen before sitting at their table with Miss Potts, the house mistress of North Tower. 'Is she new, Sally?'

'I suppose she must be.' Sally frowned, flicking her pigtails over her shoulders. 'But it's a bit strange, isn't it? I wonder why she didn't arrive with the other new girls at the beginning of term?' Malory Towers had reopened after the summer holidays five weeks ago, and it was very unusual for a new student to turn up after a term was well underway.

Darrell was intrigued. She kept an eye on the new girl as the third-formers queued up for their supper. Miss Potts, or 'Potty' as she was affectionately known, was doing most of the talking, and the new girl was listening politely, head to one side. Darrell studied her intently. She had an open, pretty heart-shaped face with very dark solemn eyes and long black plaits tied at the ends with orange ribbons.

Suddenly the girl seemed to realise that someone was staring at her. She glanced over at Darrell and flashed her a lightning-quick cheeky grin that briefly transformed her serious face.

Darrell couldn't help smiling back.

'Who's that with Potty?' Alicia Johns tapped Darrell on the shoulder, her sharp eyes having also picked up on the newcomer straight away. 'Do you know her?'

Darrell shook her head. 'No, but she looks nice.'

'Strange time to arrive, so long after the beginning of term,' Alicia observed with interest. 'Maybe there's a mystery to be uncovered there! Oh, look, it's fish for supper tonight.'

'Yuck!' Gwendoline Lacey, who was behind Alicia in the queue, pulled a disgusted face. 'I hate fish.'

'Fish is good brain food, Gwendoline Mary,' Alicia remarked lazily. 'And if anyone needs brain food, it's you!'

Gwendoline blushed angrily, but said nothing. She was afraid of Alicia's sharp tongue, and always came off worst in an argument. What she'd said was true, though, Gwen thought. It *was* extremely unusual for a student to suddenly arrive out of the blue in term time. *And* very mysterious too. Gwendoline turned her large pale blue eyes in the direction of the new girl and stared hard at her. She suddenly felt very curious indeed.

'Girls, listen, please,' Miss Potts said when everyone

was seated. 'I want you to meet Sunita Sharma. Sunita's just arrived here from India –' Gwendoline's ears pricked up. *India!* – 'and I know you'll all make her feel very welcome and help her to settle in quickly.' Miss Potts turned to Jean who was head of the third form. 'She'll be sleeping in your dormy, Jean.'

'We'll look after you, Sunita,' Jean said with a smile. She was a sensible, plain-speaking girl who was very popular, although not with Gwendoline! She was in the same dormitory as Jean, Darrell, Sally and Alicia, and Jean didn't allow Gwen to get away with *anything*.

'Thank you,' Sunita replied gratefully with another of those cheeky grins. Darrell was warming to her already. Sunita seemed very likable.

While Miss Potts remained at the table, the talk was all about Malory Towers and the activities the girls were looking forward to that term, including the half-term holiday, lacrosse matches and the Christmas concerts and plays. But when Miss Potts hurried away to speak to a group of noisy fifth-formers, the conversation turned.

'So what's the story then, Sunita?' Alicia asked bluntly, pushing her dessert bowl away and leaning forward.

Sunita opened her eyes very wide with surprise, but Darrell wasn't entirely convinced by this display of innocence. 'Story? What do you mean?'

Alicia sighed impatiently. 'I mean, why didn't you start school at the beginning of this term, like the other new girls?'

'Oh.' Sunita's gaze fell, and she stared down at the table. 'I – um – my mother was ill, and we had to wait for her to get better before we could travel,' she muttered.

Although the excuse was a reasonable one, somehow it just didn't ring true. Sunita appeared very uncomfortable and ill at ease. Frowning, Darrell glanced sideways at Sally who sat beside her. Her best friend also looked slightly disbelieving. Gwendoline, eating her own pudding, was silent, but taking in every word. *She* didn't quite believe Sunita either.

'Really?' Alicia's tone was a little cutting, which annoyed Darrell somewhat. Sunita was a new girl; they knew nothing about her background, and they ought to give her a chance at least.

Darrell decided to change the subject, and fast. She turned to the tall girl with untidy fair hair who was sitting on her other side, staring dreamily away into the distance. 'Irene, did you remember to look for that English essay you lost? You know Miss Hibbert said you'd get an order mark if you didn't hand it in tomorrow.'

'If one of us gets an order mark, it counts against the whole form,' Sally explained quickly to Sunita.

Sunita nodded, but Darrell didn't miss the look of relief that had flashed across her face when the conversation changed. And neither, Darrell could see, had Alicia.

'Just a minute, Darrell,' Irene replied absently. 'This *brilliant* tune just popped into my head.' She picked up her spoon and began to tap it rhythmically against her empty bowl. 'And one-two-three, and tum-dee-dee-dee-dum-dum!'

'Irene, you're the limit!' Alicia said, rolling her eyes. 'Look, what about that English essay? You know we'll lose our half-term if the form gets too many order marks.'

Irene stopped tapping and reluctantly focused on Alicia. 'I'm sure I gave the essay to Belinda to hand in for me—' she began.

'Ooh, no, you didn't!' Belinda, Irene's best friend, exclaimed indignantly. Belinda was a talented artist, and was as obsessed with drawing as Irene was with music.

'You wouldn't remember if she had.' Jean shook her head. 'You're both as scatty as each other!'

Irene was frowning hard with concentration. 'I *might* have left it in one of the practice rooms along with some music sheets,' she said at last.

'Let's all search for it after supper,' Darrell suggested. And maybe there'd also be a chance to talk more with Sunita, she thought. Alicia had wondered if there might be a mystery connected with Sunita Sharma's sudden appearance at Malory Towers, and Darrell was beginning to think her friend might be right . . .

'So, what does everyone think of the new girl then?' Darrell asked when she, Sally and the others finally made it to the third-form common room after supper. It had taken them quite a while to find Irene's English essay. Eventually Alicia had found the sheets of paper tucked under Irene's mattress in their dormy. 'Oh, I remember now!' Irene had exclaimed, relieved. 'The papers were a bit crumpled and dog-eared, so I stuck them under the mattress to smooth them out!'

Alicia sat down in one of the armchairs. 'Sunita's hiding something,' she guessed confidently. 'I wonder what it could be?' Sunita wasn't there as Miss Potts had taken her to see Miss Grayling, the headmistress, so the girls were able to talk freely.

'What do you mean?' asked Daphne, who was with her close friend Mary-Lou, as usual.

'Didn't you see her face when she told us that stuff about her mother?' Alicia shrugged. 'I don't think it was true. Something's definitely going on.'

'Well, *I* liked her,' Darrell said quickly. 'And I don't think we should jump to any conclusions.'

'I liked her too,' Mary-Lou agreed in her gentle voice. 'And who knows, Sunita's mother might be very ill, and that's why she's uncomfortable talking about it.' By the time she'd finished speaking Mary-Lou's cheeks were pink. Although she wasn't as much of a mouse as she used to be, she still found it hard to voice her opinions.

'Yes, let's give her a chance at least,' Sally said firmly.

'Well, I want to know what the mystery is,' Alicia drawled. 'Although I think I've already guessed . . .'

'What?' Darrell raised her eyebrows in surprise.

'I think Sunita's a princess in disguise!' Alicia announced with a grin. 'But she's decided to pretend to be an ordinary girl, just like us, while she's at school!'

There was a burst of laughter.

'A secret princess at Malory Towers?' Belinda spluttered through her giggles. 'You've been reading too many comics, Alicia!'

'Any princess in the world would be lucky to come to Malory Towers,' Sally said with a grin. 'But I don't think Sunita's a princess.'

'Yes, stop ragging, Alicia!' Darrell added, although she too was smiling. 'And anyway, even if—'

Just then the common-room door crashed open, interrupting Darrell and making all the girls turn to look. Sunita Sharma stalked into the room, head held high, nose in the air.

'Oh, would you mind shutting the door behind you, please, Sunita?' Daphne asked with a shiver, moving closer to the fire. 'It gets really cold in here if it's left open.'

'Oh, I don't close doors,' Sunita declared with a haughty glance. 'We have servants to do that at home!'

Mary-Lou scuttled over to close the door as Darrell, Sally and the others stared at Sunita in amazement. Sunita ignored them and strolled over to the fire where she stood in front of Alicia. 'I want to sit in this armchair, so please move out of my way.'

Alicia's jaw dropped. 'I *beg* your pardon?'

'I said, I want to sit here, so move!' Sunita commanded. Darrell could hardly believe her ears. Sunita Sharma was acting *exactly* like a princess – and a spoilt one at that!

Alicia's face darkened. 'Now look here—' she began.

Darrell saw Sunita's lips twitch. Then the new girl threw back her head and burst into giggles.

'Sorry,' she said through her laughter. 'It's just that I heard you talking about me being a secret princess when I was outside the door, so I decided – well, if you thought I was a princess, then I'd act like one!'

The other girls laughed along with her.

'You were very good, Sunita,' Alicia admitted. 'Are you *sure* you're not really a princess?'

Sunita grinned. 'Certain,' she said. 'I'm just as ordinary as everyone else.'

As Sunita went to join Mary-Lou and Daphne on the

sofa, Alicia felt a cold draught on the back of her neck. She turned to see where it was coming from. Mary-Lou hadn't closed the common-room door properly, and it had drifted ajar again. Alicia spotted a flash of golden hair in the narrow gap.

Gwendoline Mary listening at doors again! Alicia thought, and then a naughty idea popped straight into her head.

'Oh, you *must* take my seat, Your Highness!' Alicia jumped up and ushered a surprised Sunita into her empty chair. 'After all, a princess should be able to sit wherever she chooses! And don't worry, we won't tell *anyone* you're a secret princess. Your secret's safe with us, isn't it, girls?'

'Oh, yes!' the others chorused, joining in the joke.

'Why, thank you,' Sunita replied regally, seating herself in the armchair. 'My father the maharajah will shower you with rubies and diamonds!'

And now let's see if Gwen bites! Alicia thought to herself, dark eyes sparkling wickedly.

Outside the common-room door Gwendoline was breathless with excitement. A princess! A real live princess at Malory Towers! Gwendoline couldn't believe it. She simply *had* to make friends with Sunita. Imagine being able to tell her mother and Miss Winter, her old governess, that she was friends with a *princess*! Although she wouldn't be able to tell *everyone* because for some reason Sunita was keeping her royal title a secret. Never mind. At least the others wouldn't be able to accuse her of sucking up to the new girl. They didn't know she'd discovered Sunita's real identity.

Humming happily to herself, Gwendoline skipped off down the corridor imagining visiting Sunita in the holidays and staying in a magnificent, luxurious royal palace.

When Darrell, Sunita and the others went up to their dormy to prepare for bed, Gwendoline was lying in wait. She sprang forward eagerly as soon as Sunita came in.

'Hallo, I'm Gwendoline!' she exclaimed. 'But *you* can call me Gwen. I'm sorry I haven't had a chance to talk to you yet. How are you settling in?'

'Fine, thank you very much,' Sunita began, but then she looked taken aback as Gwendoline ushered her officiously away from the others.

'*I'll* look after you from now on,' Gwen said importantly. 'I can tell you anything you need to know, and, look, your bed's right next to mine. Isn't that wonderful? We can be best friends!'

Alicia smothered a grin as Sunita cast a bemused glance at the others over her shoulder while Gwen, still talking, led her away.

'Gwendoline Mary's playing true to form!' Alicia murmured, delighted with the success of her little trick.

'What did you say, Alicia?' Darrell asked.

'Oh, nothing,' Alicia replied, thinking she'd keep her amusing secret a little while longer.

Meanwhile Gwendoline was determined that no one else should get a look-in with 'Princess' Sunita. She kept up a running commentary about Malory Towers to Sunita all the time they were getting ready for bed, and didn't even stop talking after Miss Potts had come along to announce lights out. Jean, as head of the dormy, had been forced to speak sharply to Gwendoline as she chattered brightly on.

'We'll all get order marks if Miss Potts hears you talking,' Jean had snapped. 'Now for goodness' sake, do shut up, Gwendoline.'

Muttering indignantly to herself, Gwendoline had finally managed to quieten down. But she was very much looking forward to tomorrow, when she was dying to get to know more about her new best friend, the princess!

Meanwhile Alicia, well pleased with the success of her little plan, couldn't wait for tomorrow either.

'What on earth is Gwendoline up to?' a bewildered Darrell asked the following morning when Gwen had rushed Sunita off to breakfast before anyone else had had a chance to speak to her. 'She isn't usually so interested in helping the new girls.'

Time to come clean, Alicia thought. 'Oh, that's my fault,' she confessed airily. 'You remember when we were in the common room last night, and I pretended Sunita was a princess and gave her my chair? Well, *that* was because darling Gwen was listening outside!'

Sally gasped. 'You mean, Gwendoline thinks Sunita really *is* a princess?'

Alicia nodded, eyes bright with mischief, and the girls collapsed into laughter.

Belinda sighed. 'Oh, isn't that just like Gwen!'

'I expect she's hoping for an invitation to the royal palace,' Darrell said, chuckling. 'We'll have to let Sunita in on the joke, though, Alicia. The poor thing's looking very confused!'

After breakfast, Darrell, Alicia and Sally managed to detach Sunita from Gwendoline and take her to one side before the first class of the day began.

'I'm not sure what's going on,' Sunita confessed, very bewildered. 'Gwendoline keeps asking me what my home is like, and if I've brought any photos of it with me. Oh, and if I've got any expensive jewellery too. Why on earth has she latched on to me like this? I don't understand!'

'I think Alicia's got something to tell you,' Darrell said.

Briefly Alicia explained, and Sunita's face immediately split into a wide grin. 'Gwendoline thinks I'm a princess?' she repeated, shaking her head. 'So you mean she only wants to be friends with me because

I'm supposed to be royal? That's a bit shallow, isn't it? Sorry, I shouldn't be so rude about one of your friends, but–'

'Gwen isn't really one of our friends,' Alicia assured her. 'And she's done this kind of thing before.'

'Yes, remember when we were in the second form, and Gwendoline made friends with Daphne because she thought she was rich and grand?' Sally added.

'We can tell Gwendoline the truth right now,' Darrell added as Gwen appeared and headed in their direction, a determined look on her face, 'then she'll leave you alone.'

Sunita flashed her a wink. 'It's all right, Darrell. Leave this to me.'

'Oh, there you are.' Gwendoline hurried up to Sunita. 'Come on, I'll take you to our first class. It's French with Mam'zelle Dupont.'

'Very well,' Sunita said with a return to her haughty manner of the previous evening. Darrell's eyes widened with surprise. 'You may show me the way, Gwendoline. But please, I must request that you walk five paces in front, open every door for me and also remove any obstacles that block my path. That's how I'm treated back home.'

'Oh, yes, of course!' Gwen looked thrilled and impressed. As she hurried away to open the first door Sunita shot the other three girls a cheeky smile. Then she strolled over to the door that Gwen was dutifully holding open for her.

'Oh my!' Alicia chuckled. 'Sunita's keeping the joke going! Isn't she a sport?'

'I thought Gwendoline was going to curtsy!' Sally shook her head. 'Isn't it awful how she's always so impressed by things that don't really matter?'

Darrell rolled her eyes. 'She never learns. I wonder how long Sunita can keep fooling her?'

Darrell, Alicia and Sally followed Gwendoline and Sunita round the Court to the classroom. When they arrived Gwendoline had already saved the best seat for Sunita and, of course, was sitting proudly next to her.

'Just ask if there's anything else I can do for you,' she told Sunita eagerly.

'Open my French book, please,' Sunita commanded, so Gwen leant across and opened the textbook. Darrell almost burst out laughing when she saw the amazed expressions on the faces of Irene, Belinda, Mary-Lou and the others.

'What *is* Gwen up to?' Jean murmured, so Darrell quickly filled her in. Meanwhile Alicia was whispering to her best friend, Betty. Soon everyone in the third-form classroom knew what was going on, and they were all struggling to keep a straight face. Irene couldn't contain one of her explosive snorts of laughter, though, and had to muffle her face in her handkerchief.

A few moments later, Mam'zelle Dupont swept into the room, tip-tapping her way over to her desk on her high heels. She beamed at Sunita. 'Ah! And so we have a new girl joining us today. *Bienvenue*, Sunita.'

'*Merci*, Mam'zelle,' Sunita replied.

Gwendoline smiled. She was sure Sunita was going to be brilliant at languages. After all, a princess would be travelling the world, meeting lots of different people. And Sunita would certainly also be wonderful at music and dancing and public speaking, all the skills that a princess needed.

However, to Gwendoline's disappointment, 'Princess' Sunita turned out to be distinctly average at French. Mam'zelle clicked her tongue and shook her head when Sunita read out her translation, correcting her accent several times. Gwendoline felt a little deflated. She'd been hoping Sunita would help her with her own French exercises.

'We will now read page forty-five of your textbook together,' Mam'zelle announced.

Gwendoline immediately reached over and began to turn Sunita's pages for her. Mam'zelle saw this and almost fell off her high heels with shock.

This time Darrell couldn't hold back, and she had to laugh. So did the others. Sunita blushed a fiery red.

'Gwendoline!' Mam'zelle thundered in a very loud voice for such a short person. 'What, pray, are you *doing*?'

'I'm helping Sunita find the right place in her book,' Gwendoline muttered, scarlet-faced.

'*Est-ce vrai?*' Mam'zelle glared at her. 'And has Sunita lost the use of her own arms?'

'No, Mam'zelle,' Sunita and Gwendoline said together. By this time the class was in fits.

'Silence!' Mam'zelle ordered. 'Page forty-five, *mes enfants*, and everyone will turn their own pages with their own hands, or I shall be most displeased.'

'Oh, I thought I was going to *die* laughing!' Darrell whispered to Sally afterwards as the lesson finished and they headed to the science lab for their next class. 'Mam'zelle's face! She couldn't believe her eyes.'

'I think Sunita might start to regret keeping Alicia's trick going,' Sally replied with a knowing grin. 'You know how Gwendoline is when she gets an idea into her head!'

At that moment Sunita hurried up to them. 'Mam'zelle kept Gwendoline behind to give her another telling-off,' she gabbled breathlessly. 'Oh dear, whatever is Gwen going to do next?' Sunita pulled a comical face. 'Maybe I shouldn't have told her all that stuff about my golden palace, my diamond and ruby necklace and my favourite royal elephant called Anita!'

Alicia and Betty joined in the laughter.

'I think I'd better tell Gwendoline the truth,' Sunita added.

'Oh, don't!' Alicia begged earnestly. 'Just keep it going a little longer.'

'Yes, do, Sunita,' Betty said. 'It's *so* funny!'

'Well, all right,' Sunita agreed reluctantly. 'But if Gwendoline embarrasses me like that again, that's it!'

'Here she comes,' Darrell murmured as Gwendoline appeared in the distance and headed in their direction.

Sunita groaned. 'What class do we have next?' she asked.

'Science in the lab with Miss Myers,' Alicia told her.

'Science!' Sunita's face lit up. 'Really? I *love* science!'

Gwendoline, who was now close by, heard this, and her jaw dropped. A *princess* interested in *science*? How could that be? Princesses were supposed to love gorgeous dresses and jewellery and parties, *not* boring old science! Frowning a little, Gwen followed the others to the lab.

During their science lesson Gwendoline became even more bemused. Sunita was fascinated by the experiment they were conducting, and she hung on Miss Myers' every word. Her hand was always shooting up to answer every question the teacher asked. Gwendoline simply couldn't understand it. Although she was sitting right next to Sunita, the other girl didn't reply when Gwen whispered to her. Sunita didn't even seem to *hear* Gwendoline because she was concentrating so hard on her work. All that happened was that Gwendoline got scolded by Miss Myers for talking in class.

By the time the lesson was over Gwendoline felt thoroughly disgruntled. Sunita wasn't proving to be a very satisfactory princess at all! She packed her books away in silence, even though Sunita was chattering enthusiastically to her about how much she'd enjoyed the lesson. Darrell, who was nearby, overheard this and grinned at Sunita.

'You really impressed Miss Myers, Sunita,' Darrell said. 'You're far and away the best at science in the whole of the third form.'

'Thanks, Darrell.' Sunita glowed with pleasure. 'Science is my most *favourite* thing! I'd love to be a scientist when I grow up. It's my dream job.'

Gwendoline was so shocked she almost fainted. She stared at Sunita in astonishment. Surely a princess's job was – well – being a princess, and not a scientist!

'Um – I mean, I'd *like* to be a scientist, if I wasn't – er – going to do something else,' Sunita added hastily, noticing the stunned expression on Gwendoline's face. 'That's what I meant.'

Darrell suppressed a giggle. 'Come on, Sally and I will take you to our next lesson. It's maths with Mr Conway.'

'But we're *not* opening any doors for you!' Sally teased. She spoke in a very low voice, but Gwendoline just caught what she said. She frowned. She was so perturbed she didn't even try to catch up with Sunita as she walked off with Darrell and Sally. A nagging little suspicion had suddenly taken root inside Gwendoline's golden head. Was it possible that Sunita wasn't a *real* princess at all? Was this all some kind of trick dreamt up by Alicia and the others?

They think they're so clever, Gwendoline thought in disgust. *But I'm going to find out the truth. Then we'll see who's the clever one!*

'Oh, I did enjoy today!' Sunita sighed happily, warming her hands at the common-room fire. The girls had gathered there after supper, glad to escape the freezing foggy evening outside. 'I love Malory Towers already.'

'We all do,' Darrell told her.

'Except dear Gwendoline Mary!' Alicia said with a slightly malicious grin. 'Where is she, by the way?'

'I don't know, and I don't care!' Sunita replied with a shrug. 'She went off after supper, muttering about having something to do. I'm going to hide when she turns up!'

'Maybe it's time we told Gwen the truth,' Sally suggested.

'Oh, no!' Alicia and Betty chorused, exchanging annoyed glances. Sally Hope was *such* a goody-goody, Alicia thought crossly.

'Let's keep it going until at least tomorrow,' Betty said firmly.

Sunita hesitated for a moment, then nodded. 'All right, but do try to keep Gwendoline away from me! I want to enjoy myself at Malory Towers. I've been waiting to come here for *so* long.'

'Have you been ever to boarding school before, Sunita?' Mary-Lou asked.

'No, but I was always reading books and comics about schools just like Malory Towers before I came here,' Sunita said dreamily. 'And now it's a thousand times better than any story! Do you ever have midnight feasts? Do you have any secret societies? And do you ever play tricks on any of the teachers?'

'Play tricks? Of course we do!' Alicia scoffed. 'Anyone remember when we all pretended to be deaf in Mam'zelle's class?'

'Oh, what about the invisible pink chalk?' Darrell said, laughing. 'Betty put it all over the piano stool, and Mr Young was covered in it.'

'Then *you* put chalk on Mam'zelle Dupont's chair, but you wrote "OY!" backwards instead of just rubbing it on to the seat,' Betty recalled. 'And Mam'zelle was walking around with "OY!" on the back of her skirt!'

Sunita laughed heartily. 'Poor Mam'zelle Dupont,' she said. 'I don't think I'd like to play a trick on Mam'zelle Rougier. She's far too scary.' Sunita had met the other, stern French mistress earlier that day. 'But Mam'zelle Dupont would be *perfect.*'

Just then Gwendoline arrived outside the common-room door, but she didn't go inside. Instead she stood there silently, listening to everything the girls were saying. She was hoping to hear something that would reveal the truth about Sunita, but the others just seemed to be talking about tricks they'd played on teachers in the past.

'I've brought a trick with me that I'd love to try out on Mam'zelle Dupont,' Sunita went on eagerly. 'Look!'

Gwen peeped round the common-room door and saw Sunita produce a small glass bottle from her pocket. The contents of the bottle were a vivid violet colour.

'What is it?' Darrell asked curiously.

'I made it myself,' Sunita replied proudly. 'It's my own chemical formula. You start with ammonia and hydrochloric acid–'

'Never mind that!' Alicia exclaimed impatiently, staring with interest at the little bottle of violet-coloured crystals. 'Just tell us what it does.'

'Well, the crystals are activated with water,' Sunita explained. 'There's a delayed reaction, so you have to wait for a bit. But then the smoke begins.'

'Smoke?' Belinda repeated.

Sunita grinned. 'Yes, clouds of beautiful, violet-coloured smoke start appearing! The crystals dissolve completely, so nothing's left behind to give the game away. I'd love to hide them in the classroom next time we have French with Mam'zelle Dupont and watch her face when smoke starts drifting around from nowhere!' She stared appealingly at the others. 'Can we try it?'

'Oh, do let's!' Darrell cried, glancing at the others. 'It'd be so much fun. What do you think, Alicia?'

'I say yes!' Alicia grinned, and Betty nodded in agreement.

'Oh, Irene would love it!' Belinda predicted. 'I can't wait to tell her.'

'Where is she?' asked Mary-Lou.

'In one of the practice rooms, writing down a new tune,' Belinda replied. 'I'll go and tell her right away–'

She was about to jump to her feet, but Sally put out a hand to stop her. 'Wait a minute, Belinda. Sunita, is this smoke safe to breathe in?'

Darrell saw Alicia and Betty roll their eyes at each other.

'Oh, it's absolutely safe,' Sunita assured Sally. 'It's not dangerous at all.'

'Let's play the trick tomorrow when we have French class with Mam'zelle Dupont,' Darrell suggested eagerly. But then she saw Sally and Jean glance at each other with solemn faces.

'Look, it's nearly half-term,' Jean pointed out. 'If

we play a trick now, we might all get into trouble, and there's a chance we'd lose our half-term holiday. Then we wouldn't get to see our families, *or* be able to do any half-term activities. I vote we wait until after the holiday.'

Sally backed Jean up. 'So do I.'

'Oh, no!' Alicia pulled a face. 'Why wait? I'm longing for a good laugh! We haven't played any tricks so far this term.'

'I don't mind waiting,' Sunita chimed in. 'It'd be awful if we lost the half-term holiday. My parents are coming to see me.'

'Jean's right, Alicia,' Darrell said firmly. 'Let's wait.'

Alicia looked a little annoyed, but said no more.

'Oh, it's going to be so much fun!' Sunita said enthusiastically. 'I'm always experimenting with stuff at home, but I never get the chance to use it.'

Outside the common room Gwendoline was becoming more and more suspicious of Sunita. Would a princess *really* behave this way? Doing chemical experiments and playing tricks on teachers? It seemed highly unlikely. She *had* to find out the truth, and what Belinda had said about Irene had given her an idea. Silently Gwendoline slipped away down the corridor and headed towards the practice rooms.

'By the way these crystals are really strong,' Sunita went on, after Gwendoline was out of earshot. 'You're only supposed to use a tiny amount at a time with just a drop of water.'

'But will that make enough smoke?' asked Belinda.

Sunita chuckled. 'Yes, clouds of it!'

Meanwhile Gwendoline had found Irene in one of the practice rooms. Irene was sprawled on a piano stool, muttering to herself, trying out combinations of notes on the piano and then scribbling them down with a pencil on a music sheet. She didn't even look up when Gwendoline came in.

'Tum-tum-tee-dee, tumpty-tumpty-tum,' Irene sang, her fingers flashing over the black and white keys.

'Irene?' Gwendoline said.

Irene ignored her.

'Irene!' Gwendoline said more loudly this time.

Irene hummed under her breath, not looking round.

Gwendoline moved a little closer. '*IRENE!*'

Irene jumped a mile on the piano stool. 'Whatever are you doing here frightening me like that, Gwendoline?' she exclaimed crossly. She gave a sigh of exasperation. 'Now you've made me forget where I put my pencil.'

Gwendoline rolled her eyes. Irene had a pencil behind each ear and two more stuck in her untidy topknot.

'I was just going to say I think it's really mean of you all to pretend that Sunita's a princess,' Gwendoline said, watching Irene closely. 'It's a stupid joke, and it didn't fool me for a minute.' She waited with bated breath for Irene's reply.

'Tumpty-tumpty-tumpty-tumpty-tee!' Irene sang. Then she pulled one of the pencils from behind her ear and began scribbling furiously again.

Gwendoline felt her temper rising. '*Irene!* I know Sunita isn't really a princess, and that it's all just a *silly* joke!'

'Well, you shouldn't be such a little goose then, should you, Gwendoline?' Irene remarked absently, chewing the end of her pencil as she stared down at her music sheet. 'Imagine wanting to be friends with Sunita just because you thought she was a princess! Anyway, Alicia didn't mean anything by it. It was only a bit of fun.'

Gwendoline was furious when she heard this. It had been Alicia's idea? She might have guessed! Now that she'd found out what she wanted to know Gwendoline whirled round on her heel and stalked out of the practice room. Irene, humming under her breath, didn't even notice that she'd left.

This is all Alicia's fault, Gwendoline fumed as she marched off down the corridor. *And* Sunita's. She was so angry she didn't even notice Belinda, who was hurrying to the practice room to tell Irene all about Sunita's amazing bottle of purple crystals. Belinda was quite astonished to see Gwendoline coming out of one of the practice rooms.

What on earth's Gwen doing here? Belinda thought with a frown. *She doesn't play a musical instrument, and anyway she's tone deaf!*

As Gwendoline went to join the others in the common room her mind was racing. If only she could come up with a plan to get her own back on Sunita *and* Alicia. Gwendoline was confident that Irene wouldn't tell the others she'd found out the truth – Irene never remembered anything when she was concentrating on her music. In fact, she hardly remembered *anything* even when she *wasn't* composing! She was as scatterbrained as they come. No, Gwen had hardly any fears on that score. But she had to make her move very soon. What could she do?

When Gwendoline entered the common room the girls were still clustered round the fire. Gwen plastered a fake sweet smile on her face and headed straight towards Sunita. It was important not to let the others suspect that she'd discovered the truth.

'Here you are!' Gwendoline said brightly, sitting down next to Sunita who looked distinctly dismayed. There was a small glass bottle poking out of Sunita's pocket, Gwen noticed, and she suddenly remembered the conversation she'd overheard earlier about the smoke crystals and playing a trick on Mam'zelle Dupont.

Yes! That was it! A big Cheshire Cat smile spread

across Gwendoline's face, and she had to struggle not to laugh out loud. She'd just had the most *wonderful* idea . . .

The following morning Gwendoline crept into the classroom. She had a glass of water in one hand and a small bowl she'd borrowed from the dining-hall in the other. French with Mam'zelle Dupont was the third form's first lesson that day, which had worked out very well for Gwendoline's plan.

Gwen had been just a little worried that Irene might tell the others what she'd said in the practice room the previous evening. But as she'd predicted Irene had forgotten all about it and hadn't even mentioned it. It had been sickening having to carry on being nice to Sunita when she wasn't even a real princess, though, Gwendoline thought crossly as she opened the door of the big classroom cupboard and slipped inside. But she'd had to make sure no one suspected that she'd found out the truth.

The walk-in cupboard was filled with shelves of textbooks. Gwen moved a pile of books aside and put the bowl and glass down on the shelf. Then she took Sunita's small glass bottle of violet crystals out of her pocket. She'd stolen it from Sunita's locker the night before.

Gwendoline pulled out the stopper and poured a

shimmering stream of crystals into the bowl. *I wonder how much I should use?* she thought, pausing for a moment. But in the end she recklessly added the whole bottle. Then she tipped the glass of water over the crystals. Nothing happened and Gwendoline felt a little disappointed for a moment until she remembered that Sunita had said the reaction was delayed.

Breathing hard with excitement, Gwendoline hurried out of the cupboard. She hesitated, wondering whether to shut the door or not. But if she didn't, it might give the game away too soon, and surely the smoke would seep out through the gap at the bottom anyway? So she closed the door quietly and then darted from the classroom into the corridor. The lesson would be starting in just a couple of minutes, but at the moment there was no one around.

Gwendoline couldn't *wait* to see what would happen! The girls would assume that Sunita had gone ahead and played her trick anyway, even after Jean told her not to. They'd be *furious* at possibly missing the half-term holiday, Gwendoline thought gleefully. And even if Sunita managed to convince them that she hadn't played the trick, the others would surely blame Alicia, who hadn't wanted to wait. It was an almost perfect plan, Gwendoline decided proudly. The only *slight* flaw was that if they did lose their half-term holiday as a consequence, then Gwendoline would miss out too. But it was worth it to get her revenge, Gwendoline assured herself. And whatever happened Miss Grayling would be very angry and Sunita would be punished. Served her right for pretending to be a princess!

When the lesson began Gwendoline was on tenterhooks. She glanced at the cupboard door so often that Mam'zelle Dupont became annoyed. She thought Gwendoline was checking the classroom clock that was on the wall above the cupboard door.

'Gwendoline, this lesson will not end for another forty-five minutes,' Mam'zelle said coldly. 'If you are so very bored, then I will gladly give you extra work to do.'

'I'm not bored, Mam'zelle,' Gwendoline replied hastily. She hadn't even started working on the sentences that Mam'zelle had given them to translate from English into French. She'd been too intent on watching for the first signs of smoke. But there'd been nothing yet.

'Then you have already finished the translation I set you?' Mam'zelle fixed Gwendoline with her beady black-eyed stare. 'Come, share your work with us. The first sentence is *I ate bread, butter and cheese for lunch*. Now, *en français, s'il vous plaît*!'

Groaning inwardly, Gwendoline got to her feet. She'd written nothing down, so she'd just have to try to do it from memory. '*J-J'ai mangé*,' she stammered hesitantly, '*du paon*—'

'*Paon?*' Mam'zelle wrung her hands and rolled her eyes dramatically. '*Oh, là, là*, Gwendoline! Your accent, it is atrocious! I tell you before – one, two million times – *pain* is bread and *paon* is peacock. See, two different sounds, *ne sont-ils pas*?' She raised her eyebrows. 'Do you eat peacock for lunch, Gwendoline?'

The class giggled.

'No, Mam'zelle,' muttered Gwendoline, trying not to sneak another glance at the cupboard. Secretly she thought Mam'zelle had rather a cheek criticising her French accent when the teacher's own English accent left a lot to be desired!

Mam'zelle waved impatiently at Gwendoline to sit down, and she did so thankfully. She'd better concentrate from now on, Gwen thought, bending her head over her books, or she'd end up with extra work. Sunita had probably been boasting about those silly crystals all along, just to make out she was better at science than she really was! She'd have to think up a new plan. Gwen sniffed in disgust as she picked up her French dictionary.

It was Darrell who noticed the first wisps of violet-coloured smoke. She'd finished translating the sentences, put her pen down and raised her head. It was then she noticed a very faint purple mist drifting from the gap at the bottom of the cupboard door. Darrell blinked, thinking it was just a trick of the light. But when she looked again more smoke was floating lazily out.

Darrell's quick brain instantly made the connection. *Sunita's crystals!* she thought. She nudged Sally, who sat next to her, and silently pointed at the cupboard door. Sally's eyes widened and she gasped softly.

'I thought Sunita agreed not to play the trick until after half-term,' Sally whispered.

'So did I,' Darrell whispered back. 'Jean's going to be really annoyed.' She glanced at Sunita, who was sitting not far off, and tried to attract her attention. But Sunita, head bent over her work, didn't notice.

Wisps of smoke were now beginning to seep out all round the doorframe, and some of the other girls had begun to notice it too. As Gwendoline smiled smugly to herself Alicia whispered to Betty, and Belinda nudged Irene. Daphne stifled a giggle and pointed the smoke out to Mary-Lou. Darrell could see that Jean had spotted it too. She looked extremely annoyed, and Darrell could understand why. What was going to happen when Mam'zelle Dupont noticed the strange-coloured smoke? It really was the most vividly bright violet colour that Darrell had ever seen! She felt laughter bubbling up inside her. She couldn't help it.

The purple smoke curled and swirled further into the room. Mam'zelle had noticed nothing so far, and Darrell had to bite her lip to stop herself from giving the game away. Irene couldn't control herself, though. Hastily she whisked out her handkerchief and snorted loudly into it.

Mam'zelle jumped in her seat, very startled. 'Irene, *ma pauvre petite*, what ails you? You are snizzing very strongly. Ah, this chilly English weather! Do you have the cold in the head?'

Irene gasped as a little cloud of violet-coloured smoke drifted across the room straight towards the French teacher. 'No – I mean, yes, Mam'zelle!'

Darrell glanced at Sunita who'd obviously only just realised what was happening. She was sitting bolt upright, a look of utter confusion on her face.

I don't think Sunita played the trick after all, Darrell decided quickly. *She looks too surprised. So who could it be?* She turned to look at Alicia. She and Betty had their heads together, giggling as they watched the drift of smoke waft itself directly under Mam'zelle's nose.

The whole class held its breath. Suddenly Mam'zelle Dupont spotted the smoke curling around her and let out a shriek. 'Help! *Aidez-moi!* I am on fire!'

'You're not on fire, Mam'zelle; it's just smoke!' Darrell tried to explain, but by now she was laughing so much she could hardly speak.

Mam'zelle Dupont leapt up from her chair. 'I have heard your English saying that there is no smoke without fire!' she cried, peering suspiciously under the desk and then behind her chair. Everyone in the room was laughing helplessly now, even Jean and Sunita, and Irene was almost weeping into her handkerchief.

Then Mam'zelle spotted the smoke seeping from the closed cupboard door. 'So, here is the fire!' she exclaimed, pointing at the door. 'We must evacuate the classroom, *mes enfants*, and fly for our lives!'

'*Flee* not *fly*, Mam'zelle!' Alicia spluttered, her sides aching with laughing so hard.

Mam'zelle suddenly looked highly suspicious. 'But why is there no heat? No flames?' She advanced cautiously towards the cupboard door. 'I see only smoke. Aha!' She clapped her hands together triumphantly and glared at the girls. 'Now I understand. This is a *treek*, is it not? You have played another of your *treeks* on your poor Mam'zelle!'

'But, Mam'zelle, none of us have been inside the cupboard,' Betty pointed out.

'We shall see!' Mam'zelle retorted impressively. 'I, Mam'zelle Dupont, will discover the origin of this so-purple smoke. And if it *is* a terrible *treek* –' she grasped the door handle – 'then you shall all be punished most severely.'

Mam'zelle flung the cupboard door open. Instantly a huge cloud of purple smoke came billowing out, enveloping her from top to toe. The smoke was so thick the class couldn't even *see* the French teacher. They could just hear her coughing.

'You – will – all – take an order mark!' Mam'zelle croaked through her coughs. 'Two, no, *three* order marks each! And you will write lines! Many, many lines! A thousand lines each! *We must not play treeks on Mam'zelle Dupont!*'

Purple smoke was still pouring out of the cupboard, and within a couple of minutes the whole classroom was full of it. Darrell could barely see Sally, who was sitting right next to her, through the haze of violet. They both began to cough.

'Open the doors and windows!' Darrell heard Jean shout. 'Hurry!'

Feeling rather scared, Gwendoline rushed to open the window closest to her. She hadn't expected so much smoke. It was rather frightening. *Still*, she comforted herself gleefully, *it just means that Sunita will get into even more trouble.*

Coughing, some of the girls climbed up on to the chairs and tables and tried to waft the smoke out of the open windows by flapping their French textbooks to create a draught. No one was laughing now as they shouted encouragement to each other. Meanwhile Darrell dashed to open the classroom door. Leaving it wide open, she grabbed her French book, climbed up on to a chair and began flapping at the smoke with the others. It was clearing quickly now, and through the thin haze Darrell saw Mam'zelle Dupont totter over to her desk and collapse into her chair, still coughing.

'What is the meaning of this commotion?' asked a calm authoritative voice from the doorway.

The noise ceased as if by magic, and everyone, including Darrell, froze. *Miss Grayling!* She could see the headmistress's tall, familiar figure through the thinning smoke.

Quickly the girls scrambled down from the chairs and tables. Gwendoline's heart was thudding wildly as she scurried back to her place. Miss Grayling waited and did not speak again until everyone was seated.

'Who is responsible for this?' she asked quietly.

Sunita stood up. 'I am, Miss Grayling,' she said in a trembling voice.

'Very well,' Miss Grayling replied. 'Come with me, Sunita. Jean, please fetch Mam'zelle Dupont a glass of water. The rest of you will proceed quietly to the hall and wait there until the smoke has cleared. You will stay late this afternoon to make up for the lesson time you have missed.'

Gwendoline had to struggle not to smile triumphantly as Sunita, looking very pale, left with the headmistress. Her clever plan had worked out even better than she'd expected.

Sunita's knees shook as she stood in front of Miss

Grayling's desk. When she'd arrived at the school the headmistress had told her that she hoped Sunita would be one of Malory Towers' successes and learn to be 'good-hearted and kind, sensible and trustable'. Sunita didn't feel like any of those things at the moment.

'Let us deal with the most important thing first,' Miss Grayling said. 'I assume you concocted whatever mixture created that purple smoke?'

Sunita nodded, very embarrassed.

'Is it dangerous? Is Mam'zelle Dupont's health at risk, or any of the girls', including yourself?'

'Oh, *no*, Miss Grayling!' Sunita replied so earnestly that the headmistress believed her without question. 'My father helped me make the smoke crystals – you know he's a scientist – and neither of us would *ever* do anything to harm anyone.'

'And did your father know that you intended to use these smoke crystals at school?'

Sunita flushed. 'No, Miss Grayling,' she muttered.

'I see.' But Sunita wasn't at all prepared for Miss Grayling's next question. 'So it was you who set up the trick?'

Sunita was caught. She didn't know exactly who had stolen her bottle of crystals, although she suspected Alicia. But she wouldn't have sneaked to Miss Grayling anyway, even if she'd known for sure. Should she just *pretend* that she was the culprit? Sunita didn't want to lie to the headmistress, but on the other hand, if she 'confessed', then maybe the other girls wouldn't lose their half-term holiday.

Miss Grayling observed the girl in front of her very closely and guessed something was wrong. 'Sunita,' the headmistress said quietly, 'is there something you ought to tell me?'

'No, Miss Grayling.' Unable to look the headmistress in the eye, Sunita stared down at the floor. 'It's all my fault.' Secretly Sunita comforted herself with the thought that at least this was true. If she hadn't brought the crystals to Malory Towers, this morning's disaster would never have happened.

'Sunita?' Miss Grayling leant forward in her chair. 'Did someone take the bottle of crystals and play the trick without your knowledge?'

Meanwhile the girls had gathered in the school hall. Mam'zelle, clutching a glass of water, had staggered off to the staffroom to sit down.

'What on earth was Sunita thinking?' Jean said angrily. 'We agreed not to play the trick before half-term. She ignored us!'

'And Sunita herself told us it only needed a tiny amount of crystals and a drop of water to make lots of smoke,' Belinda pointed out. 'She must have used the whole bottle!'

Gwendoline hastily smothered a nervous giggle. She hadn't known the chemical crystals were *quite* so powerful.

'Do you think we'll lose our half-term holiday?' Mary-Lou fretted.

'I don't think it was Sunita who played the trick,' Darrell blurted out. The others turned to glance at her in astonishment, and Gwendoline felt slightly uneasy. 'She was as surprised as the rest of us when she spotted the smoke,' Darrell continued. 'Honestly, I'm sure it wasn't Sunita.'

'Then who was it?' Sally asked soberly.

Jean and Darrell both glanced at Alicia. 'No, it *wasn't* me!' Alicia snapped. 'I know I didn't want to wait until after half-term, but do you *really* think I'd be so stupid as to use the whole bottle of crystals after Sunita warned us not to?'

'No,' Jean agreed quickly. 'I believe you, Alicia.'

'Me too,' Darrell agreed. 'But if it wasn't Alicia, then who was it?'

By this time Gwendoline was seriously alarmed. Things were getting out of hand! She had to turn the situation round somehow. Quickly she spoke up. 'Well, I think it *was* Sunita!' she declared. 'How terrible! I mean, to think that a princess could behave in such an awful way! I know it's supposed to be a secret that Sunita's really a royal princess, but I couldn't help overhearing you talking to her, and that's how I found out.' Gwendoline was pretty pleased with herself. As long as everyone thought she still believed Sunita was a princess, and her friend, then they couldn't *possibly* suspect Gwen herself of being the culprit who'd stolen the crystals. Gwendoline preened herself slightly. How clever she was!

'Don't be a little goose, Gwendoline Mary,' Alicia said impatiently. 'Sunita isn't a princess. It was just a joke, and you fell for it.'

'Oh!' Gwendoline clapped a hand to her mouth as if she was surprised, but really it was to hide a little smile. 'You mean – she's just an ordinary girl like the rest of us after all?'

'Yes.' Alicia grinned maliciously at her. 'I don't suppose you'll want to be friends with her any more now, will you?'

'I certainly *don't* want to be friends with Sunita Sharma any more whether she's a princess or not,' Gwendoline replied haughtily. 'I still think she played that trick, and now it might have cost us our half-term holiday.'

Suddenly Gwendoline noticed that Irene was staring at her, a perplexed expression on her face. Gwen gulped, her heart pounding uncomfortably as she wondered what Irene was going to say.

'I thought you knew Sunita wasn't really a princess, Gwendoline,' Irene remarked, frowning.

'No, of course I didn't!' Gwendoline blustered. She was highly relieved when Irene said no more. The others didn't really take any notice. They were far more interested in discussing whether Darrell was wrong and Sunita *was* actually to blame.

'Maybe Sunita just thought it would be funnier if she used the whole bottle,' Jean suggested.

'And perhaps she looked surprised when Darrell glanced at her because she wasn't expecting quite so much smoke,' Daphne added.

'Or maybe *Alicia* decided to use all the smoke crystals for a joke,' Gwendoline remarked gleefully, glad of the chance to pay Alicia back. 'After all, we know how much she loves playing tricks.'

'I already told you, it wasn't me!' Alicia retorted. But Gwendoline could see that some of the girls were giving Alicia sidelong looks again. By now Gwen was supremely confident that she was absolutely off the hook until Belinda, who'd been whispering to Irene, suddenly spoke up.

'Gwendoline, why did you go to the practice room last night?'

Gwendoline faltered. 'Wh-what?'

'I saw you coming out of one of the practice rooms yesterday evening,' Belinda continued. 'Why did you go to talk to Irene?'

Gwendoline gasped, feeling her carefully constructed

plot come tumbling down around her ears. 'I didn't!'

'Yes, you did,' Irene said suddenly. 'I remember now. You said you knew that Sunita wasn't a princess and it was all a silly joke!'

All eyes now turned towards Gwendoline.

'It was *you*!' Darrell said slowly. 'You set the trick, didn't you, Gwendoline?'

'I suppose you were trying to pay Sunita and me back for playing that joke on you?' Alicia murmured, disgusted.

'No wonder Mam'zelle told you off for staring at the cupboard all the time, Gwendoline,' Sally remembered. 'You were watching for the smoke to appear, weren't you?'

'It wasn't me,' Gwendoline began nervously, but Jean was staring sternly at her.

'Come along, Gwendoline,' she said in a grim voice. 'We're going to see Miss Grayling immediately.'

'No, I won't!' Gwendoline muttered tearfully. But after a few moments, as all the girls stared at her in silence, she reluctantly followed Jean out of the hall. A babble of chatter broke out after they'd gone.

'So it was Gwendoline all along!' Betty shook her head in disbelief.

'Isn't Gwen silly?' Darrell sighed. 'Now she's probably lost her own half-term holiday, along with the rest of us.'

'Oh blow, is that what you think will happen?' Irene asked anxiously. 'I wish I'd remembered earlier what Gwendoline said to me in the practice room. I'd completely forgotten until Belinda jogged my memory just now.'

'We'll just have to wait and see what Miss Grayling decides,' Sally said anxiously.

Meanwhile, in Miss Grayling's study, a scarlet-faced Gwendoline stood with Jean and Sunita in front of the headmistress, having confessed to everything. Mam'zelle Dupont was also present. Miss Grayling had sent for the French teacher earlier to see if she had any idea whom the real culprit could be, now she was convinced Sunita was not to blame.

'I am seriously displeased with you, Gwendoline,' Miss Grayling remarked frostily. She had particular concerns about the way Gwendoline continually latched on to anyone who appeared rich or grand in any way, and resolved to discuss it with her privately later. 'It was a very reckless thing to do, and I must think seriously about an appropriate punishment.'

Gwendoline bit her lip.

'Oh, please, Miss Grayling, don't let the other girls miss their half-term holiday!' Sunita pleaded, wondering where on earth she'd found the courage to speak up when she was shaking like a leaf. 'They had nothing to do with it, and anyway it isn't *all* Gwen's fault. I shouldn't have brought the smoke crystals to school with me, and I shouldn't have pretended to be a princess. It was a silly thing to do.'

Miss Grayling thought for a moment. 'Mam'zelle, what do you think?'

'Ah! These naughty girls!' Mam'zelle cried, shaking her head. She'd had time to calm down now, and she'd very much enjoyed recounting the dramatic tale of the lurid-coloured smoke that had appeared from nowhere to some of the other teachers. 'It was a very bad *treek* to play, but I truly believe that at heart they are fond of their Mam'zelle Dupont! I would not like to deprive them of the chance to see their families at half-term.' Sunita's heart leapt, and even Gwendoline looked hopeful. 'But perhaps some extra French lessons for Sunita and Gwendoline during the holiday?' Mam'zelle suggested. She glanced at Miss Grayling who nodded.

'Oh, *thank* you, Mam'zelle!' Sunita said fervently. They were getting off lightly, she knew. Dear Mam'zelle Dupont! How kind she was.

Gwendoline, on the other hand, struggled not to scowl. Extra French lessons when everyone else would be enjoying themselves? It would be unbearable!

'Come, Gwendoline, try to contain your delight, *mon enfant*,' Mam'zelle remarked slyly, knowing full well how Gwendoline was feeling. 'We will work hard on your French accent. Never shall you eat peacock for lunch ever again!'

'Oh!' Darrell cried out with delight. 'Here's my mother and father at last!'

It was the start of the half-term holiday, and a familiar black car was coming slowly up the long drive to join the others already parked round the school building. Darrell shot out of the doorway where she'd been waiting impatiently, sidestepping the other girls who were milling around greeting their own parents, and ran to meet Mr and Mrs Rivers.

'I thought you were never coming!' Darrell said happily, embracing her pretty mother, then her tall, dark-haired father. 'I've got *so* much to tell you.'

'Hallo, darling,' her mother said with a smile. 'I *am* glad to see you looking so marvellously well!'

'Hallo, Darrell, my dear.' Mr Rivers hugged his daughter in return. 'How are you? Have you been behaving yourself? Not been playing too many tricks, I hope?'

'Of course not, Daddy!' Darrell turned pink. She hadn't told her parents about Sunita's smoke crystals yet. It would be a funny story to tell them over lunch perhaps.

'Well, well, well!' Darrell's father had just noticed the car that had travelled up the drive behind them. It was a long, sleek black limousine, and it was driven by a chauffeur wearing a smart grey uniform and a peaked cap. 'I wonder who this can be?'

At that moment Darrell saw Sunita rush across the drive towards the limousine. 'Mum! Dad!' Sunita was yelling excitedly. 'It's so good to see you!'

Darrell watched as Mrs Sharma, wearing a beautiful green sari shimmering with gold embroidery, climbed gracefully out of the car. She embraced Sunita warmly. They were joined by Sunita's father, a tall, distinguished-looking man with a calm, kind face.

'What a charming family!' Mrs Rivers remarked. 'Is she a new girl, Darrell?'

'Yes, that's Sunita Sharma,' Darrell replied. 'She's in our form. She's lovely.'

Gwendoline too had noticed the expensive car Sunita's parents had arrived in. As she walked past with her mother and her old governess, Miss Winter, Gwendoline cast a glance full of bitterness at her. All this terrible extra French study was *her* fault! And now look at Sunita, showing off with her chauffeur and her expensive car, Gwendoline thought enviously. Miss Grayling had spoken very seriously to her about not being dazzled by the money and possessions that other girls had, and had advised choosing her friends based on their good qualities instead. Well, even if Sunita was the Queen of England, Gwendoline wouldn't want to be friends with her *now*!

'Did you say this new girl's name was Sharma?' Mr Rivers asked Darrell quietly when Mrs Rivers had turned away to speak to Mrs Hope, Sally's mother.

'Yes,' Darrell replied, wondering why her father was staring so keenly at Mr Sharma as he stood chatting to Sunita.

'Her father, Sunil Sharma, is one of the most famous scientists in the world,' Mr Rivers told his daughter. 'I've seen him featured in my medical journals more than once. That's how I recognised him, from the photographs. He's a remarkable man, very intelligent and compassionate.'

Darrell gasped. 'I know Sunita loves science, but she never mentioned a word about her father.'

Mr Rivers nodded understandingly. 'I believe he's quite often engaged in work that's top secret,' he said. 'That may be why she hasn't said anything.'

Later that day, Darrell managed to grab a moment alone with Sunita in the dormy after their parents had left.

'My father recognised yours, Sunita,' Darrell told her. 'He said he was a famous scientist and a remarkable man!'

Sunita glowed with delight. 'Did he? How nice of your father to say so!' She lowered her voice. 'My dad's working on a secret project for the UK government at the moment. It all happened really suddenly, and it's so secret even my mother and I don't know what it's about. That's why we're here, and that's why—'

'You couldn't explain the real reason why you started at Malory Towers so late in the term,' Darrell chimed in. 'Mystery solved! Don't worry, Sunita, I won't say a word to anyone, not even Sally. But does that mean you'll go back to India when your father's work is finished?'

Sunita nodded. 'That's why I want to enjoy every minute of my time at Malory Towers!' she exclaimed. She dipped into her pocket, pulled out a small paper bag and offered it to Darrell. 'Here, Darrell, have a sweet.' Darrell took one of the round white sweets and popped it into her mouth. It tasted pleasantly fruity and creamy when she bit into it.

'I just wish Gwendoline hadn't taken the smoke crystals,' Sunita continued with a sigh. 'She ruined what would have been a brilliant trick.'

Darrell just couldn't resist. 'Don't you have any other tricks up your sleeve?' she asked naughtily.

Sunita shrugged. 'Look in the mirror, Darrell,' she said solemnly.

Darrell glanced in the mirror. Her lips looked rather a strange colour, she thought, puzzled. They seemed to have turned slightly blue. Darrell opened her mouth, peered inside and then jumped backwards in amazement.

Both her tongue and her teeth were the brightest blue she'd ever seen!

Darrell gasped. 'What's happened to me?'

'Sorry, Darrell.' Sunita collapsed into giggles. 'You ate one of my special trick sweets! Don't worry – the colour will wear off in fifteen minutes or so.'

Darrell burst out laughing. Even if Sunita only spent a short time at Malory Towers, it was going to be so much fun having her around!

The Show Must Go On

by Rebecca Westcott

'Isn't it terrific to be back?' said Darrell Rivers, settling down in the lower fourth common room at Malory Towers. It was after supper on the first day of term and all the girls were tired, their stomachs nicely filled with the fantastic spread that was always laid on for the first evening. Next to her Sally groaned contentedly.

'Absolutely. Although it's a good job that Cook doesn't prepare meals like that every day because I don't think I'd be able to get anything done if I was always feeling this full.' She rubbed her tummy appreciatively, making Darrell laugh.

'Well, I for one wish that the food was always as good as it is on the first night,' said Gwendoline Mary from the other side of the room. 'I've eaten like a queen this holiday and I'm really going to miss all the wonderful food that Miss Winter and Mother ordered for me. You wouldn't believe it – I've had salmon and real cream and–'

'Oh, do be quiet,' snapped Alicia from her perch on the window seat. 'We've all eaten well in the holidays but you don't hear us going on about it, do you?'

'No, but my food was—'

'So, what are we going to do for the fourth-form showcase, Darrell and Sally?' interrupted Alicia, while Gwendoline sulked silently in the corner and asked herself for the hundredth time why her father insisted on sending her to a school where the girls were so rude and ill-mannered. 'Have you had any thoughts, because I've had *tons*.'

Darrell glanced at Sally and then back at Alicia, feeling a little bit nervous. She liked the other girl a great deal but it was no secret that Alicia had a sharp tongue and an even sharper brain – and as head girls of the form Darrell didn't want her and Sally to lose control of the showcase before they had even begun.

'We've had a few ideas,' she started. 'Sally and I wrote to each other in the holidays and we've started hashing out a plan. It's all in hand, Alicia – you don't need to worry.'

'Although we'd be very happy to hear everyone's ideas, wouldn't we, Darrell?' added Sally, giving Alicia an easy smile. 'Miss Grayling says that we need to put on a presentation that shows how wonderful life is here at Malory Towers and we really want to do the very best that we can.'

'Shall we have a meeting tomorrow?' asked Alicia, pulling the curtains closed. 'Say, four o'clock in here? We need to get started right away if North Tower is going to have the best showcase. I've heard that West Tower started rehearsing last term, but then again they've got Betty for head girl and she is an *extremely* good leader.'

The following afternoon Mam'zelle Dupont stood at the front of the classroom and clapped her hands at the start of the last lesson. 'Settle down, girls! Goodness me! You 'ave all returned from the 'olidays like a bunch of young – 'ow do you say? – 'oodlums!'

'What is an 'oodlum, Mam'zelle?' asked Alicia, her face a picture of innocence. 'Is it an animal?'

'Oh, yes, I think it is!' joined in Belinda, as keen as Alicia to delay the start of the lesson. 'In fact, I'm pretty sure that I saw one in the holidays when my people took me on a day trip to the zoo!'

'No, no, no!' called Mam'zelle. 'You 'ave not understood me. I said that you are like a bunch of 'oodlums!'

'Yes, that's what I saw at the zoo,' confirmed Belinda. 'A great, big, bunch of 'oodlums. They were hanging around in the treetops, swinging from branch to branch.'

'What did they sound like?' asked Irene, pushing her glasses up her nose and grinning at Belinda. 'Was it something like this?'

She started making an awful screeching noise, making Mam'zelle clasp her hands over her ears.

'Stop it! Stop it, you 'orrible girl! You will be bringing Miss Potts in 'ere if you keep on making that terrible sound and I do not want 'er to tell me that my class is making too much noise on the very first day of term!'

Darrell was laughing so much that it was hard to take a breath, but eventually, once she had calmed down, she turned to the rest of the giggling girls and shook her head.

'We have to be quiet,' she told them. 'If Miss Potts *does* come in, then she'll probably give us all some extra work and we won't be able to have our meeting about the showcase. So just settle down for goodness' sake!'

'Ooh, our mighty head girl has spoken,' muttered Alicia. 'Everyone had better stand to attention.'

Darrell frowned but before she could reply Sally's hand rested on her arm.

'That's exactly what being head girl is all about,' she whispered as Mam'zelle regained control of the room and started putting verbs on the board in her scrawled handwriting. 'Sometimes we have to say the thing that nobody else wants to say, but if it's for the right reason then that's all that matters.'

The lesson passed slowly. Mam'zelle Dupont gave them verb after verb to conjugate and the fourth-formers' heads were reeling by the time the lesson ended and they staggered into the common room.

'We might as well start the meeting now,' said Darrell,

glancing around the room. 'Everyone seems to be here.'

'So, what are we actually doing for this showcase then?' asked Gwendoline. 'Because I've told my people that it's going to be amazing and Daddy is going to be driving all the way from London so that he can bring Mummy and Miss Winter. They're so excited about seeing me perform!'

'And what exactly is it that you're going to be performing, dear Gwendoline Mary?' asked Alicia, flashing a wicked grin at Darrell. 'I'm sure that we'd all love to hear your contribution.'

'Erm, I'm not really – er, I don't think that . . .' blustered Gwen, her cheeks going red. 'I haven't really . . .'

'Got any ideas?' finished Alicia, her voice sweet. 'Now, that *is* a surprise because you're normally so forthcoming with excellent suggestions.'

'Tell us about *your* ideas, Alicia,' interjected Darrell. She found Gwen as irritating as everyone else did but she could see the girl's discomfort and it didn't seem right to let Alicia rib her for too long.

'Oh, right.' Alicia turned away from Gwen. 'Well, I was thinking that we should do something really spectacular!'

'OK.' Darrell's voice was wary. Spectacular sounded like it might be quite difficult to achieve but she had promised to listen and so listen she would.

'Picture the scene!' Alicia leapt to her feet and spun around, her arms out wide. 'A darkened stage. A single spotlight. And then, out of the gloomy depths, comes a troupe of tumbling acrobats! They juggle with fruit! They conjure doves out of thin air! They pull rabbits from hats. And then, just as the audience thinks that it can't get any better, there is a clap of thunder and they all disappear as rapidly as they arrived!' She looked around the room at the captivated faces before her. 'What do you think?'

'It sounds magical!' breathed Mary-Lou.

'Incredible!' gasped Irene.

'Inspired!' murmured Belinda.

'Impossible,' stated Darrell, breaking the spell. 'You're the only one who can juggle and tumble, Alicia, and I don't know how Sally and I are supposed to find doves and rabbits. And even if any of us knew *how* to do magic, I don't think Miss Grayling would be too happy about us turning Malory Towers into a zoo, do you?'

'Spoilsport,' muttered Alicia, rolling her eyes. 'Come on then. What other ideas have you all got?'

'I thought we could put on an opera,' offered Irene. 'I've already got the music written and I could easily teach you the words. It would be wonderful – I can see it all in my mind.' She closed her eyes. 'We'll have a lighthouse and an ocean and everyone will be dressed like mermaids and you'll emerge from the water, singing in beautiful harmony together.'

'Are *we* meant to be making this lighthouse?' whispered Darrell to Sally, staring at Irene in disbelief. 'And none of us can sing apart from Mavis. It'll sound less like a mermaids' choir and more like a cats' chorus.'

'That does sound wonderful,' said Belinda loyally. 'Although I was thinking about something a bit more artistic. I wondered if we could create an exhibition? You know, to display all of the brilliant artwork that we do here at Malory Towers!'

'You mean, the brilliant artwork that *you* do,' said Alicia, scrunching up her nose. 'The rest of us can't draw or paint for toffee. And the showcase is supposed to involve everybody.'

Darrell leant forward. 'Alicia is right. We can't have a presentation that is all about one person. Whatever we choose, it has to be with all of us.'

Alicia grimaced. 'Well, I don't envy you and Sally for having to choose,' she told Darrell. 'I can't think of a single thing that we can *all* do unless our showcase is about having midnight feasts, getting into trouble with Miss Potts and playing pranks on Mam'zelle – and I don't think North Tower is going to have the best presentation with any of those things!'

* * *

All week Darrell spent every spare minute racking her brain for good ideas and imploring the rest of the lower fourth to put their thinking caps on. But while everyone had plenty of thoughts about what they could do to highlight their own talents and skills, there was nothing that could involve the whole class. Darrell was starting to feel desperate about the whole thing when something happened that put all thoughts of the showcase out of everyone's heads.

'Have you heard?'

The voices were calling over each other as Darrell and Sally walked into the common room.

'There's a new girl! She's coming tomorrow and her name is Margaret!'

Darrell looked at Sally in surprise. It was unusual for a new girl to arrive once term had started.

'I overheard Matron talking to Miss Potts,' said Mavis. 'She said that the poor little mite was due here tomorrow and then Miss Potts said that it was all very sad.'

'What did she mean?' asked Sally, looking concerned. 'Why is it sad?'

'I don't know.' Mavis shrugged. 'Perhaps she–'

Before she could continue, Alicia came bursting through the door. 'There's a new girl coming here tomorrow!' she shouted, skidding into the room.

'We know,' Belinda told her. 'Her name is Margaret

and apparently she's a *poor little mite*, according to Matron.'

'Well, I bet you don't know *this*!' Alicia paused to catch her breath, casting a look around the room as she did so. 'Good. She isn't here.'

'No, she's coming tomorrow,' Darrell said. 'You just told us that.'

'I didn't mean *her*.' Alicia grinned at Darrell. 'I know the new girl isn't here yet. I was talking about the new girl's cousin!'

'What are you on about?' asked Belinda, looking confused. 'Are you saying that the new girl has a cousin at Malory Towers?'

Alicia looked smug. 'That's exactly what I'm saying.'

'Oh, crikey.' Mary-Lou looked worried. 'It isn't *my* cousin that's coming here, is it? She's terribly mean. I have to see her once a year at Christmas and she always teases me and calls me a little mouse.' She shudders. 'I couldn't bear it if she was the new girl.'

'You *are* a little mouse,' Alicia told Mary-Lou. 'And no, you daft thing. Don't you think your parents would have told you if your cousin was coming to Malory Towers?'

'Oh, yes, you're right!' Mary-Lou looked relieved. 'Thank goodness for that!'

'So whose cousin is it?' asked Darrell, rather feeling that the conversation was heading in the wrong direction.

'It can't be any of ours because you said that the person wasn't in the room.'

'I'll give you a clue,' Alicia smirked, enjoying the attention. 'She is very delicate and ever so important and if she doesn't brush her beautiful golden locks at least one hundred times a night then the world will stop turning.'

There was a pause as the girls looked at each other in disbelief.

Darrell spoke up. 'You don't mean Gwen, do you?'

Alicia nodded and the room filled again with the sound of voices.

'You mean to say that Gwen's cousin is coming here? To Malory Towers?'

'You're pulling our leg, Alicia. This is another one of your tricks – it has to be!'

'I didn't even know that Gwen had a cousin.' The last voice was Mary-Lou and it silenced the room. None of the other girls ever really paid much attention to Gwendoline and her boastful comments but there was a time when Mary-Lou had been close to her. And if *she* didn't know about the existence of a cousin then that was odd because Gwen loved talking about herself and her family more than any other subject.

'Well, she *does*,' stated Alicia firmly. 'Darling Gwendoline Mary Lacey has a darling cousin and she will be starting in the lower fourth tomorrow.'

'No wonder Matron called her a *poor little mite*,' said Darrell, wincing. 'Imagine being related to Gwen.'

'Never mind that,' Alicia told her, looking grim. 'What if this relation of Gwendoline Mary is as selfish and puffed up and vain as she is? One of her is bad enough.'

'And there's going to be two of them,' whispered Mavis, her face dropping. 'What are we going to do?'

The next day, all anyone could talk about was the new arrival. The girls tried to ask Gwen about her cousin but she was surprisingly reluctant to talk.

'It's extremely strange,' Darrell told Sally as they walked along the first-floor corridor. 'I'd have thought that Gwen would revel in telling us every last detail of her wonderful cousin but she's hardly told us a thing.'

'Well, we won't have to wait much longer,' said Sally, pausing at the big picture window that overlooked the drive. 'Unless I am mistaken Gwen's parents are getting out of that car, which means the girl behind them must be Margaret. I wonder where her own parents are?'

The two girls peered eagerly out of the window, desperate for a first glimpse of the new girl. Outside, Mr Lacey was lifting up a battered old trunk while Mrs Lacey fussed about with an umbrella, which was refusing to go up. They could hear her squeals of dismay as the rain fell on to her immaculate and ornate hair and Darrell grinned, thankful once again for her own sensible and practical parents who had never once given her cause for embarrassment.

'I can't see Gwen's cousin properly,' complained Sally, standing on her tiptoes. 'Although she definitely has blonde hair.'

'I wonder if she's as vain about it as Gwendoline is?' said Darrell. 'Oh, bother – there goes the bell for supper. I suppose we shall just have to wait to see.'

As everyone ate their meal Darrell and Sally shared what they had seen.

'I wonder why her own people didn't drive her down?' said Alicia, spreading some butter on a slice of bread. 'Most parents would want to bring their daughter themselves.'

'Perhaps they're very important and have been called away on urgent business abroad,' mused Mavis. 'That might explain why she has to start partway through the term.'

'Or maybe they just couldn't be bothered.' Alicia jerked her head to the far side of the table, where Gwen was sitting alone. 'Let's face it – Gwendoline's family aren't exactly known for their kind and considerate nature, are they?'

'Alicia,' protested Darrell, feeling that the conversation had gone too far. 'We don't even know the new girl yet. It isn't right to judge her *or* her family before we've seen what she's like for ourselves.'

'Well said,' whispered Sally as Alicia scowled and turned away. 'Everyone deserves a chance – Alicia should know that. Goodness, she's had more than enough second chances over the last few years!'

Once supper was over, the girls made their way back to the lower fourth common room and settled down. Mary-Lou and Mavis took a jigsaw puzzle from the cupboard and sat at the small table. Darrell and Sally curled up on the sofa and started chatting quietly about their plans for the showcase, while unbeknown to either of them Belinda started sketching them both, her clever pencil perfectly capturing the look of concentration on their faces. Irene paced the room, humming to herself and occasionally beaming with delight when she found the right note for her song.

'Miss Potts is heading this way!' called Bill, pushing the door open and making everyone look up. 'And she's got the new girl with her.'

'Have you been in the stables all this time?' asked Darrell, glancing at the clock. 'Goodness me, Bill – if old Potty had caught you, then you'd be in trouble! You know that you're only allowed twenty minutes after supper to say goodnight to Thunder.'

'Do I look presentable?' asked Bill, frantically smoothing down her dress. 'Do I look as if I've been sitting calmly in the common room with you all?'

'Only if the common room has suddenly turned into a farmyard,' Alicia told her drily, plucking a piece of straw out of Bill's hair and thrusting a book into her hand. 'There! You look positively serene and studious now.'

Darrell was still laughing when the door opened and Miss Potts stepped inside.

'Good evening, girls,' she said, casting her eye around the room and narrowing them slightly when she saw the mud on Bill's shoes. 'This is Margaret. She is to be in your form and I'm sure that you will all give her a warm welcome.'

She moved to the side and a very tall girl stepped out from behind her. Sally had been right – she did have blonde hair that was exactly the same colour as Gwen's but that was where the similarity ended. Darrell cast her a curious look, searching for a likeness between the cousins but struggling to find any.

Gwen liked to wear her hair in long, flowing waves down her back but Margaret's hair was short and straight, cut into a practical bob just above her shoulders. Both girls had blue eyes but Margaret's dark blue reminded Darrell of the Cornish sea when a storm was brewing – very unlike Gwen's pale blue eyes that forever gave the impression that she was about to burst into tears.

Darrell glanced across the room to where Gwen was

skulking in the corner. Surely she would greet her cousin? But Gwen didn't move. She didn't even offer a smile. Instead she picked up her book and buried her nose deep inside the pages, which was interesting because Darrell knew that Gwen would usually work very hard not to have to read anything.

'I'll leave Margaret here to get acquainted with you all,' said Miss Potts, her eyes flickering towards the corner where Gwen was steadfastly ignoring the whole situation. 'Please remember that starting at a new school can be quite a difficult time. I expect all of you to help her settle in as quickly as possible.'

Then she turned and walked back through the door, leaving Margaret standing alone in the middle of the room.

'Hello,' said Darrell, feeling like she should be the first to speak. 'Welcome to Malory Towers and the best house in the school!'

Margaret looked at her but didn't say a word. She turned slowly, taking in everything before her. The beautiful old wooden beams. The slightly worn but comfortable furniture. The huge fireplace.

'We're allowed to have fires in the winter term,' Belinda told her, putting down her sketchbook. 'It's ever so snug in here then.'

But Margaret didn't appear to be listening. Instead her eyes had alighted on the girl in the furthest corner of the room and she stood very still, gazing at her with a look that Darrell couldn't interpret.

'Hallo, Gwendoline.' Finally she spoke and her deep, quiet tone was so different to the sharp, shrill voice of her cousin that Darrell had to suppress a gasp.

'Hallo, Margaret.' Gwen put down her book and stood up, casting her eyes over the girl in front of her. 'I see that Mother and Miss Winter found some of my old school uniform for you. It's not really your size, is it?'

Everyone looked more closely at Margaret. She was wearing the ill-fitting uniform awkwardly, the look not improved by the scruffy brown boots on her feet.

The girl shrugged. 'It's clothes,' she replied. 'Who cares whether they fit or not? And my name is Maggie, as you very well know.'

Gwen laughed. 'Oh, dear! I'm afraid that you're at Malory Towers now and you need to start behaving like a proper young lady.' She flicked her hair so that it hung over one shoulder. 'And proper young ladies are not called silly nicknames like Maggie! I rather thought that Mother and Miss Winter might have explained that to you?'

'And I rather thought that your mother and governess might have explained that a proper young lady isn't rude or snide or unfriendly,' retorted Margaret. 'But I can see that you haven't changed a bit since I last saw you.'

Gwen stood up, her eyes blazing. Darrell shifted in her seat but Alicia caught her eye and shook her head.

'Better let them sort it out,' she whispered. 'And besides, we can't stop this now!'

'And I can see that you haven't changed either!' spat Gwen. 'You're still the common, uncouth, unsophisticated girl that you've always been but I don't know why I'm surprised, considering who your parents are.'

The room stilled. Margaret's fists clenched by her side and both Sally and Darrell stood up. They didn't know what was happening but Gwen had surely gone too far.

'Shall we show you to your dormy?' asked Sally, her voice shaking. She was an excellent leader but she hated conflict and the tension in the common room was so thick that it felt like a heavy fog hanging in the air. 'It's really lovely.'

'What is that supposed to mean?' Margaret's words were quiet and her eyes bored into Gwen. 'What *about* my parents?'

'I expect your trunk has been taken upstairs by now,' said Darrell, slightly desperately. She could see that Alicia was loving every second of the confrontation but there was something about Margaret's voice that was making Darrell feel increasingly nervous.

'Oh, you know very well!' Gwen clearly wasn't about

to back down. 'My mother married up and your mother married down and that is why I am who I am and you are, well –' she gestured at Maggie – '*you*.'

There was silence and the rest of the girls held their breath. They were used to arguments between them but they'd never heard anybody say anything so personal and unkind before.

'I'd rather be me with my wonderful parents, than spoilt darling Gwendoline Mary,' murmured Margaret, her face pale. 'There isn't enough money in the world that would make me ever want to swap places with you.' She turned and let her gaze sweep over them all. 'I wouldn't want to be like *any* of you. Not even for one day.'

And then she turned and ran from the room, her long legs striding across the floor and out of the door before anyone could stop her

Over the next few days Margaret and Gwen refused to be in a room at the same time unless it was absolutely unavoidable. During classes Margaret sat at the side of the room with a hard expression on her face while Gwen sat in her usual place at the back where she constantly hoped that no teacher would call upon her to answer any questions. When the girls had free time Margaret would roam the grounds in her scruffy brown boots, hands stuffed into her pockets and her head bowed, clearly deep in thought.

The boots were becoming a bit of a problem. There was a very strict uniform code at Malory Towers and every girl had to wear exactly the same thing. A smart white blouse with a brown pinafore dress over the top and practical black shoes on their feet. Margaret had already been given two order marks by Miss Potts for wearing the boots but when Sally tried to talk about it with her she just turned and walked away, which made the other girls cross.

'What Gwen said about Margaret's parents was unforgivable,' said Darrell to Sally as they walked out to the lacrosse pitch one evening after supper. 'And to make such a big thing about her having to wear Gwen's old uniform too – I knew that Gwen could have a mean tongue but I've never heard her sound so nasty before. But Margaret isn't helping herself either. It's like she just doesn't want to be here.'

'It's a bad business all right,' agreed Sally. 'Look – there's Margaret now. Let's catch her up and see if we can't show her that Malory Towers isn't full of stuck-up girls like her cousin.'

'Margaret! Hey – Margaret!' yelled Darrell. 'Wait for us!'

Ahead of them the girl kept walking. Darrell looked at Sally in surprise.

'Maybe she didn't hear us?' ventured Sally, although

the expression on her face showed that she didn't really believe that.

'Well, I've had enough of this frightful atmosphere,' said Darrell. 'This needs to be sorted once and for all. We've still got the showcase to organise for goodness' sake. There's no time for all this horridness.'

Breaking into a run, she sprinted towards the tall girl, Sally right behind her.

'Hi, Margaret! Shall we show you the way to the lacrosse pitch?' Darrell panted once she'd reached her side. 'Have you played before?'

Margaret stopped and turned to face them. It was immediately obvious that she'd been crying.

'Are you OK?' asked Sally, worried. 'If there's something wrong then you can tell us. Darrell and I are joint head girls and we'll try to help. We know how hard it can be, starting at a new school.'

'You can't help *me*,' snapped the girl, rubbing her eyes fiercely with her hands. 'Unless you can perform miracles, and I don't think that even you *amazing* Malory Towers girls can do that.'

Darrell blinked, taken aback at the bitterness in her voice. 'What do you mean?' she asked.

Margaret laughed but it wasn't a happy sound. She waved her hand, gesturing at the glorious old school building, the bricks glowing red in the setting sun. 'You all think that you're something special just because you go to school here. You think that this is normal but it isn't. It isn't normal to spend your afternoons swimming in a pool next to the sea. It isn't normal to have all your meals cooked for you and your clothes washed for you while you swan around the place, riding your ponies and sketching in art books.'

Her voice was getting louder and starting to attract the attention of the other girls, who drifted closer to see what was going on.

'Look here, Margaret–' began Darrell, feeling rather ruffled by the new girl's rudeness about Malory Towers. But she couldn't say anything more before Margaret uttered a shriek of frustration and stamped her scruffy brown boot on the grass.

'My name is *not* Margaret!' she shouted. 'It's Maggie and I don't care if that isn't upmarket enough for any of you because I don't want you to talk to me anyway.'

'I've told you before, you can't use that ridiculous name here,' Gwen said, appearing from behind them, a sly look on her face. 'Mother and Miss Winter said that it was foolish of your father to shorten your name like that and that maybe now he's dead the silly nickname can die too.'

There was a stunned silence for a second and then, with a cry of anguish, Margaret threw her lacrosse stick on the ground and took off, running like the wind across the lawn and disappearing out of sight round the side of the school.

'Well!' Gwen's voice was dripping with satisfaction. 'I think you can all see what I mean now. She doesn't come from the right sort of people and the sooner that Miss Grayling understands that the better. In fact, I may even write to Father tonight and tell him that Margaret is letting down the family name.'

'Don't you dare,' said Darrell, her voice shaking. 'If anyone is letting people down, then it has to be you. Is it true, what you just said? About Maggie's father having died?'

Gwen nodded, seemingly unaware of the sea of angry faces before her.

'He died very suddenly and left his family with nothing.' She rolled her eyes and sighed dramatically. 'The only reason that Margaret is here at Malory Towers is because of *my* father's generosity. He and Mother went straight to her house when we heard the news and offered to pay for her school fees. Her mother didn't want her to leave but as Mother said, she wasn't really in a position to look a gift horse in the mouth!'

'No wonder she doesn't want to be here,' whispered Sally, her eyes filling with tears. 'She's lost her father and now it must feel as if she's lost her mother too. Poor, poor Maggie.'

'Oh, don't you start using that name too,' said

Gwen sniffily. 'Mother and Miss Winter say that it really is very common and that people like them should make more of an effort to pull themselves up by their bootstraps.' She laughed suddenly. 'And you all know *why* she wears those horrible boots, don't you?'

The other girls were silent, which Gwen took as a signal to keep talking.

'It's because she hasn't got any others! Mother dug out some of my old school uniform for her to wear but my shoes didn't fit her so she's stuck with the boots. Isn't that a hoot! She's here at Malory Towers wearing *my* old clothes and using *my* old trunk. It's a good job she's never learnt to swim or she'd be having to borrow my old bathing costume, no doubt – and imagine how embarrassing *that* would be!'

'Just be quiet!' shouted Alicia, her face red. 'You should have told us that she was having such a difficult time. We could have tried to help her and instead you let us think that she hated us all.'

'You are a spiteful, selfish girl, Gwendoline,' added Darrell. 'And Maggie is very unlucky to have you as a cousin.'

The other girls nodded and Darrell cast a concerned look towards the school. How on earth was she supposed to bring everyone together when there was so much unhappiness in the lower fourth?

* * *

'It's just no use,' said Darrell the next afternoon after another showcase meeting. 'Everyone has got brilliant ideas but we can't do them all and we can't choose just one of them because Miss Grayling specifically said that every single one of us has got to be involved.'

'Why can't we do them all?' asked Alicia, from the window seat. 'That would keep everyone happy. We could have a showcase that involves everyone's ideas.'

'How are we supposed to do that?' asked Darrell, frowning. 'You want us to have a diving contest and Belinda wants an art exhibition. Irene wants an opera and Bill thinks that we should have a horse-riding show.'

'And you want us to put on a lacrosse demonstration,' sighed Sally. 'You're right. It's an impossible task.'

'But what if it wasn't?' said Alicia, her eyes sparkling. 'What if we could show all of these things in one afternoon? Wouldn't that be splendid!'

'What do you mean?' asked Belinda from her place on the rug. 'How can we do all of those things in the auditorium?'

'It wouldn't work at all,' added Irene, stopping her humming. 'Bill's horse would eat Belinda's paintings and you can't exactly dive on to the stage, Alicia!'

'But we wouldn't *be* on the stage,' said Alicia, leaning forward. 'You're all thinking far too small.' She stood up and started pacing the room. 'Just imagine it. We could start off down at the swimming pool and then, once we've shown our diving skills we could take the audience to the auditorium where the artwork would be displayed. And next we could head to the pitches and see a lacrosse game and then end up at the stables for a demonstration about horse-riding!'

'That would take all day,' said Sally, shaking her head. 'The showcase isn't supposed to be more than thirty minutes and it's definitely got to be staged in the auditorium.'

Everyone groaned and Alicia sank back down on to her seat.

'So, we're back to square one,' muttered Mavis. 'This is a disaster.'

'No, it isn't,' said Darrell suddenly. 'Alicia is on to something. We *can* show all of those things *and* we can do it in half an hour!'

'Well, I don't see how,' grumbled Gwen. She was sitting in the corner and as usual Maggie was nowhere to be seen. 'And I hate all of those ideas. I'm not good at any of those things and my parents are driving all this way to watch me perform.'

'Then they're going to be very disappointed, because you aren't good at anything,' snipped Alicia. 'Now do be quiet and let us hear what Darrell has to say.'

Gwen's cheeks went red but she did as she was told and Darrell continued.

'The reason we've been struggling to come up with

one idea for the showcase is because there are so many brilliant things for us to show,' she explained. 'So let's do what Alicia said. Let's show everything that is wonderful about Malory Towers as a series of still-life scenes. You know, like living pictures where we pose on the stage in different positions!'

There was a moment of silence while the girls all contemplated her words and then their voices joined together in excited chatter.

'That's a brilliant idea!'

'Could it work? I think that it might!'

'We could use props to help us show each scene!'

'Oh, well done, Darrell! Well done!'

Darrell beamed around the room. 'It was Alicia's idea really,' she said. 'I can't take all the credit.'

'Hip hip hooray for Darrell and Alicia!' sang Irene, grabbing hold of Belinda's hands and pulling her up from the floor. 'North Tower is going to have the best showcase that Malory Towers has ever seen!'

Once a plan had been made, the showcase quickly started to come together. Darrell and Sally sat down with Belinda and she sketched each scene so that they could discuss exactly how it should look. When this had been agreed, they all got to work making costumes and rehearsing exactly how it should be staged.

'The showcase is coming along really nicely,' Sally

said to Darrell as they walked to the gymnasium the following week. 'The main problem now is how to get Gwen and Maggie involved. I can't get them to agree on anything.'

'Can't they just welcome in the parents or something?' asked Darrell, not really listening. Mam'zelle Dupont had promised them a dance lesson today and while Darrell usually excelled at physical activities dance was definitely not her strong point.

'We can't leave them out.' Sally's face was wrinkled with worry. 'Miss Grayling specifically said that everyone has to be included.'

'Well, Gwen will just have to come and hold a lacrosse stick and be part of my still-life scene,' said Darrell, telling herself that it was sacrifices like this that made for being a decent head girl. 'And Maggie can join in too.'

Sally sighed. 'You know Gwen won't do anything sporty, even if it *does* only involve standing still. And as for Maggie, well, she doesn't do anything wrong but she still won't talk to any of us and whenever the subject of the showcase comes up she always seems to disappear. I just don't know what to do about her.'

'I suppose it must all seem very frivolous and unimportant,' said Darrell, as they entered the changing room. 'After what has happened to her I expect the last thing she wants to think about is our showcase. Perhaps we should just leave her alone and let her stay out of it?'

'Yes, I suppose so.' Sally put her bag down on a bench. 'It's just that my mother always says that distraction can really help when things are tough-going.'

Inside the gymnasium Mam'zelle was winding up the gramophone. 'We are going to start with some free movement,' she called as the girls entered the room. 'I want you all to listen to the music and move around the space, letting the music lead your feet. Poor Gwendoline has a terrible 'eadache and so she will not be dancing today. Instead she will sit quietly in the corner and watch the rest of you.'

She looked across at Gwendoline, who smiled bravely back at her.

'Funny how she always seems to have a headache when we have dancing lessons, isn't it?' whispered Alicia to Darrell. 'She was just the same last year. It's because she knows how rubbish she is.'

The music began and everyone except Gwendoline started to dance.

'No, no, no!' called Mam'zelle after a few seconds. 'Darrell Rivers! This music is not about the circus so why are you dancing like the elephant? *Tiens!* I 'ave never seen anything like it in my life!'

'I'm trying my best,' muttered Darrell through gritted teeth. 'It isn't my fault if I have two left feet. Daddy says that I take after him.'

'Just wiggle your arms up and down,' hissed Alicia, flapping past Darrell. 'She likes it if you move your whole body.'

Darrell gave Alicia a grateful smile and continued around the room, making her arms quiver in the air.

'*Alors!*' screeched Mam'zelle. 'What is this now? Darrell, are you trying to be a flying elephant? Is this a joke you play on me, you 'orrid girl?'

Across the room Alicia took one look at Darrell's frustrated face and burst out laughing. Her giggle was infectious and before Mam'zelle could stop them most of the girls were bent double, clasping their stomachs as they roared with laughter at Darrell's elephant dance.

'That is quite enough!' shouted Mam'zelle. 'You will all come over 'ere and I will tell you exactly what I think about your 'orrendous English dancing.'

Still sniggering, all of the girls made their way to the front of the hall. Almost all of them anyway.

There, in front of them, was Maggie. She was still wearing the same tatty old boots that she refused to take off, despite the fact that Miss Potts had got wind of the situation and provided her with a perfectly fine pair of school shoes that would fit. Not that the boots were slowing her down. As the music sped up so did Maggie, twirling and whirling as if she hadn't heard a word anyone else had said. The girls watched, open-mouthed, as she spun around the room, her arms flowing as if she was in water and her long legs leaping higher and higher before landing so gracefully that the heavy boots didn't make a sound on the wooden floor.

Eventually the music ended and the girls broke into rapturous applause. Maggie looked up, shocked, as if she hadn't realised that they were there.

'That was amazing!' yelled Belinda, dashing across the hall. 'We didn't know that you could dance!'

'Neither did I,' said Maggie softly. She looked down at her feet as if in disbelief. 'We didn't do dancing at my old school.'

'You looked like a magnificent butterfly,' said Irene as the rest of the girls rushed to Maggie's side. Gwen got up from her seat and followed them slowly.

'Yes – your butterfly dance was definitely better than Darrell's elephant dance!' added Alicia, giving Darrell a wicked grin.

Darrell scowled at her and then gently placed her hand on Maggie's arm. 'That was wonderful,' she told her. 'Really. I've never seen anyone dance like that. Say that you'll be part of a dancing scene for our showcase!'

'Oh, yes – please do!' clamoured the other girls.

Maggie looked down at Darrell's hand on her arm and then back up at the kind, caring face before her. 'I don't really know if–' she began, but the rest of her words were drowned out by a louder voice.

'That's a completely ridiculous idea!' Gwen stepped

forward and gave a loud sniff. 'I hardly think that our parents are coming all this way to see someone like *her* stand on stage in her hand-me-down clothing and scruffy old boots, do you?'

'Shut up!' barked Alicia but it was too late. The door to the gymnasium was swinging open and Maggie was nowhere to be seen.

'Why are you so cruel to her?' shouted Darrell, her eyes narrowing. 'That was a horrible thing to say!'

'That's quite enough!' called Mam'zelle Dupont, clapping her hands loudly. 'I don't know what has got into you all but there are some very ill-tempered girls in the lower fourth today. We will not dance while you are all so unfriendly.'

She waved her hand theatrically in the air. 'I suggest that you all go and get some fresh air before suppertime and try to make peace with one another.' And then, muttering under her breath, she swept out of the gymnasium, leaving Gwen surrounded by a class of angry girls.

'You heard what Mam'zelle said.' Alicia turned to face Gwen. 'You need to go and find Maggie and apologise to her for being so unkind.'

'And you have to tell her that we all think she should take part in the showcase,' added Darrell. 'Including you. Otherwise you're going to make her think that nobody wants her to be here.'

'I *don't* want her to be here!' cried Gwendoline, her face going red. 'Nobody asked *me* whether I was happy for her to come to *my* school and be given *my* clothes! Mother and Father spent days talking about *poor Margaret* and what was to be done, but nobody asked my opinion, not once!'

'That's it,' said Darrell slowly as everything slid into place. 'That's why you're so unkind to her. You're jealous of your own cousin, even after everything that she's been through.'

The gymnasium fell silent as everyone contemplated Darrell's words.

'I would have said yes if they'd only asked but they were too busy worrying about *her* to think about me.' Gwendoline looked up at Darrell, her eyes swimming with unshed tears. 'I know you all think that I'm a terrible person.'

'You *are* pretty terrible,' agreed Alicia. 'I've been saying it for a while.'

'No, not terrible, not really,' said Sally, shaking her head. 'You're just not very good at thinking about others. That makes you a bit selfish, but not terrible.'

The girls looked at each other as Gwen stood quietly, her head bowed and her shoulders slumped. She looked thoroughly miserable and defeated, which was not a look they had ever seen on Gwen before.

'It's just that our families have never really got on but

now she's all that Mother and Father can talk about,' she murmured, sounding very small. 'I suppose I felt a bit pushed out. I know I've been horrible to her.'

'You can make it right, though.' Darrell gave Gwen a serious look. 'You need to find her and tell her that you're sorry.'

Gwen nodded and walked towards the door. 'I hope it's not too late,' she said, her voice subdued. And then she was out in the sunshine and gone from sight.

'Does anyone fancy going down to the pool?' asked Alicia after a few moments of silence. 'I'm going to take Mam'zelle's advice and get some fresh air.'

A few girls murmured their assent and Darrell nodded. 'I think a long swim would do me good,' she agreed. 'I need to wash away the taste of all that horridness.'

'I'll meet you down there!' said Alicia as they left the changing rooms and headed across the lawn in the direction of the dormitories.

Alicia was already at the pool by the time Darrell got there, laying out her towel on the warm rocks that ringed the water.

'I'm going to dive in,' said Alicia. 'Care to join me?'

She gestured to the high diving platform and Darrell nodded. Together the two girls climbed the ladder and then, once they had reached the top, they paused for a moment to take in the view. It truly was a wonderful sight with the sea stretched out before them and the sunshine glistening on the waves.

'Who's that?' Alicia peered towards the small area of sand that divided the rocks from the sea. 'It looks like Gwen but why on earth would she be down there? She hates the sea – she says it's too cold and wet for her, the silly goose.'

They both stared at the distant figure.

'It looks like she's shouting something,' said Darrell. 'What *is* she doing?'

And then the words floated over to them on the sea breeze, so faintly that to begin with Darrell thought she was imagining things.

'Help! Please help!' Gwen's voice was filled with fear. 'Someone come quickly and help us!'

'What does she mean, help *us*?' frowned Alicia. 'She's the only person there. I expect she's got sand in her shoe or something else equally ridiculous.'

'No, Alicia – look!' Darrell pointed further out to where a sand spit reached into the sea. There, waving her arms wildly, was the figure of another girl.

'It's Maggie!' declared eagle-eyed Alicia. 'And the tide has cut her off from the land. Well, she's going to have a wet journey home! Do you remember when I had to swim out from there last summer? It wasn't easy, I can tell you.'

Darrell did remember. No girl was allowed to swim

in the open sea on this part of the coast but before that incident with Alicia they sometimes enjoyed going for a paddle. After that day Miss Grayling had banned all the girls from walking out on to the sand spit because, as Sally had said at the time, if a strong swimmer like Alicia almost got into difficulties then it would be incredibly dangerous for anyone else to risk getting caught.

And Darrell also remembered something else. 'But, Alicia!' She turned to the other girl, her eyes wide open in fright. 'Have you forgotten what Gwen said the other day? Maggie can't swim!' The two girls leapt into action, scampering back down the ladder and slithering over the rocks as fast as they possibly could, ignoring the bumps and scrapes that they were getting as they made their way down to where Gwen was standing. She turned as they approached, her face pale with fear.

'It's Maggie!' she said, pointing out towards the narrow strip of sand. 'The tide is coming in so quickly and she can't swim, Darrell – she can't swim!'

'We need to get help,' said Darrell. 'Quickly, Gwen – run back up to school and tell Miss Grayling to telephone for the coastguard.'

Gwen didn't hesitate. She ran as fast as she could, ignoring the longer path that wound its way up to the school and instead scrambling the shorter route over the seaweed-strewn rocks that led directly to the swimming pool.

Darrell watched her for a second, amazed at the speed and determination in her actions, and then turned back to speak to Alicia. But the other girl was already heading straight for the water's edge.

'What are you doing?' called Darrell. 'The tide is coming in – we need to wait for help.'

'There's no time!' Alicia pointed to where Maggie was still waving. The sand spit was no longer visible and the water was up to Maggie's knees. 'If we wait, she's going to be under the water in a matter of minutes.'

And with that Alicia waded out into the sea and dived forward, her strong arms cutting through the water and propelling her towards the stricken girl.

Darrell looked anxiously back at the rocks. Gwen was almost at the pool but she still had to run from there up to the school and there was no telling how long the coastguard might take. Alicia was right – if Maggie was going to be saved then it was going to have to be *them* that saved her, even if that meant breaking one of Miss Grayling's most important rules.

Running forward, Darrell gasped as the cold water hit her body. But she wasn't going to let Alicia go out there alone and so, pulling on all her courage and strength, she started to swim.

The waves crashed over her and she spluttered as she

tried to keep a straight course and catch up with Alicia. But the other girl was by far the stronger swimmer and every time that Darrell looked up Alicia was pulling further and further away.

Time seemed to slow down and the only thing that Darrell could focus on was each stroke of her arms.

You can do it, she thought to herself. *Just keep going. You've got to get to Maggie.*

And then, finally, she was there. Reaching down with her feet, she stood on the sand and looked anxiously around. Maggie was standing ahead, the water already up to her waist, and Alicia was talking to her urgently. Darrell waded across to join them.

'We've got to go,' Alicia said. 'The tide is coming in really quickly now. If we don't leave then the water is going to be over our heads in a few minutes.'

'But I can't swim.' Maggie was shivering, whether with cold or fear Darrell couldn't tell. 'I only came out here for a paddle and then the sea cut me off before I knew what was happening.'

'It's going to be fine,' Darrell told her. 'Alicia and I will look after you but you have to do exactly as we say, OK?'

Maggie shook her head. 'No. I can't do it.'

Alicia groaned in exasperation. 'We can't wait for help. There's no other way.'

Darrell took in Maggie's tear-stained face and

terrified eyes. 'You have to trust us,' she said, her voice as calm as she could make it. 'We won't let you go, Maggie. I promise.'

Maggie paused and stared at Darrell as if she was making a difficult decision. And then she nodded.

'Tell me what to do,' she whispered.

And so the three girls waded out to the edge of the sand spit. Darrell and Alicia sank into the water, their legs kicking wildly to keep them in place.

'Lower yourself in and let us support your shoulders,' called Alicia. 'Some water might splash on to your face but we won't let you go under.'

Maggie crept forward with shaking legs and the girls reached out, pulling her down until she was floating between them.

'We've got you,' shouted Darrell above the roar of the waves. 'Now kick like fury, Maggie! Kick harder than you've ever kicked in your life!'

It was tougher than they could possibly have imagined. Darrell and Alicia each pulled themselves through the water with one arm, holding tightly to Maggie with the other. The wind picked up and the waves seemed to throw themselves relentlessly at the girls as they splashed furiously towards the land. The only bonus was that the tide was their friend this time, pushing them ever forward and finally, delivering them in a heap on to the sand.

'Girls! What on earth has been going on!' cried Miss Grayling, hurrying down the cliff-path with Miss Potts and Gwendoline close behind her. 'I was told that there was a lower-fourth-former stuck out on the sand spit!'

'Not any more,' said Alicia, gasping. 'We rescued her.'

Miss Grayling took in the scene before her. The three soaking-wet, bedraggled girls were all kneeling on the beach, struggling to catch their breath, and she leapt immediately into action.

'Gwen! Run and tell Matron to cancel the coastguard and then to prepare hot drinks and warm blankets. Miss Potts, we need to get these girls up to the school and into some dry clothes as quickly as possible.'

Gwen cast an unseen but desperate look at her cousin before darting off. Darrell and Alicia pulled themselves to their feet and followed behind as Miss Potts put her arm round Maggie and gently started to lead her towards the school.

'That was an incredibly irresponsible thing that you both did,' murmured Miss Grayling, as the wet, exhausted procession made its way up the cliff-path.

'But, Miss Grayling–' began Alicia and Darrell in unison, but the headmistress put her hands on their shoulders and stopped them.

'It was irresponsible but it was also brave,' she continued. 'You may well have saved a life today, girls. And while the very thought of all three of you being in danger makes me shudder, I am immensely proud of your bravery and selflessness. There are some people in the world who run away from a crisis and others who run towards it, looking for ways that they can help. You are both fine examples of the latter.'

And even though Darrell was so cold and tired that it was difficult to take another step, Miss Grayling's words seemed to warm her up from the inside and give her legs enough energy to make her way towards the hot chocolate and cosy beds that were awaiting them all.

It didn't take long for Darrell and Alicia to recover from rescuing Maggie, which was just as well because the days just seemed to fly by. Darrell was so busy that she didn't know whether she was coming or going between the usual lacrosse matches and practices, making sure that all her schoolwork was done and planning the showcase with Sally.

'Everything is looking wonderful,' Sally announced one evening. The girls were gathered in the common room for the weekly meeting. 'Alicia, your diving scene is absolutely marvellous!'

'Thanks!' Alicia grinned. 'But it's a team effort. It wouldn't look half as good if the other girls weren't doing their bit!'

'And your artwork is stunning,' Sally continued, looking across the room at Belinda. 'It was so kind of

Miss Linnie to let us have the easels from the art room.'

'We just need to work out how to finish the show,' said Darrell. 'The still-life scenes are fantastic, but it would be nice to have something a bit different for the grand finale.'

'We have to keep thinking,' Sally said. 'And we still need to find a scene for Maggie and Gwen.'

'Where *is* Maggie?' asked Darrell, peering around the common room. 'And Mary-Lou, come to think of it?'

Irene laughed. 'Where do you think they are? In the gym of course!'

The girls all grinned. As soon as she had recovered from her ordeal in the sea, Maggie had been spending most of her time dancing in the gymnasium, the faithful Mary-Lou always on hand to work the gramophone. It seemed that after her awful shock Maggie was somehow less miserable at Malory Towers. The first thing she had done when she was allowed out of bed was to find Darrell and Alicia and ask to speak to them alone. Nobody else knew what the three girls had talked about and neither Darrell nor Alicia could be persuaded to discuss it, but Maggie, while still subdued, was starting to become friendly with almost everyone in the lower fourth.

Everyone except Gwen, that is. The relationship between the two cousins was as cold as ice and even though the rest of the girls could see that Gwen was feeling wretched about the whole thing, Maggie refused to talk to her.

Darrell wondered whether she should try to get involved but Sally advised her against it.

'They need to sort it out in their own time,' she told Darrell. 'And at least Maggie has her dancing now.'

It was true that dancing seemed to have unlocked a side to Maggie that nobody had seen before and it made the lower fourth glad to see that there was one thing about Malory Towers that made her happy.

And Maggie seemed to have unlocked a side to Gwendoline Mary that nobody had seen before either. The previously selfish, mean-spirited girl had started to demonstrate a kinder personality that came as quite a surprise to the rest of the form.

'I've just seen something very odd,' said Mavis one afternoon, a week after the sand spit incident. She glanced around the common room to make sure that neither Gwen nor Maggie was there and then sank into a seat. 'I was coming back from my singing lesson and Gwen was loitering about by Maggie's dormy with a package in her hands and looking very suspicious. So I held back and watched her and then, when she was sure that there was nobody around she darted into the dormy and when she came back out the package was gone!'

'Ooh, very mysterious!' teased Alicia. 'What could it possibly mean?'

They all laughed and forgot about the whole thing until later when Maggie walked in, looking puzzled.

'Does anyone know who put these on my bed?' she asked. In her hands was a pair of brand-new dance pumps. 'My name was written on the package but I haven't ordered them.'

'Well, yes – that must be what–' started Irene, but Alicia rushed to interrupt her.

'We haven't got a clue,' she said firmly. 'Maybe they were sent from home?'

Maggie shook her head. 'I don't think so,' she said, sounding doubtful.

'Well, I'd just enjoy them,' said Alicia, shaking her head surreptitiously at the others. 'Are they the right size?'

Maggie sat down on the floor and pulled the pumps on. They were a perfect fit.

Darrell wasn't sure what was going on but the opportunity seemed too good to miss.

'I don't suppose you'd consider changing your mind about the showcase, would you?' she asked Maggie, crossing her fingers behind her back.

Maggie looked up. 'Now I've got the right shoes, I suppose I could,' she said shyly. 'If you still want me to?'

'Of course we do!' said Sally. 'That's fantastic – you've solved the problem of what we can do to end the show. Irene can compose the music and you can choreograph a dance. It'll be wonderful!'

The room buzzed with enthusiasm and Maggie stood up, her eyes shining.

'I might go and practise now,' she said. 'I want to come up with something that will make you all proud! Thank you, everyone.'

As soon as she was out of the room, Darrell looked at Alicia.

'Why didn't you tell her that the dance pumps were from Gwen?' she demanded. 'Now she thinks that one of us gave them to her and that's not very fair.'

Alicia leant back in her chair and grinned.

'It wasn't for us to tell her,' she said. 'Gwen clearly didn't want to make a big thing of it, which quite honestly is the most surprising thing that has happened this term. If she wants Maggie to know, then she'll tell her and until then we have to keep out of it.'

The day of the showcase finally arrived. Darrell woke early, having spent half the night awake, worrying that the Cornish weather might prove to be against them, but she shouldn't have been concerned because when she threw back the curtains the sun was already high in the sky and there wasn't a cloud in sight. The parents would all be able to enjoy a traditional Malory Towers high tea on the lawn after the showcase!

The morning was busy and all too soon it was time for lunch.

'I'm far too jumpy to eat a thing,' complained Irene as they walked down the corridor. 'I feel like there's a family of frogs living in my tummy.'

Sally smiled at her. 'Your music is marvellous, Irene,' she told her. 'What could possibly go wrong?'

'Oh, don't say that!' moaned Irene, her face going white. 'I'm sure that I'm going to forget a note or mess up the timing or something.'

'You'll be fine,' reassured Darrell. 'Hey there – Maggie! Are you ready for today?'

Maggie was ahead of them, deep in conversation with Mary-Lou. She turned now and gave Darrell a wave.

'I think so,' she called. 'Although I'm feeling ever so nervous!'

'You're going to be brilliant!' shouted back Darrell. 'We'll meet you by the stage at three o'clock, OK?'

Maggie nodded and Darrell turned to Sally, a big grin on her face. 'She seems so much happier now,' she said. 'I know that it must still be very strange for her, being here and not at home, but she's really settled into Malory Towers.'

'Between being rescued from the sea by you and Alicia and discovering that she can dance, I'd say that she's come a long way in the last few weeks!' Sally said, laughing. 'And I hope that after today Maggie is going to feel as if she completely belongs here with us.'

Darrell smiled happily, but then hesitated as she remembered that not everyone's problems had been solved this term. The more that Maggie seemed to grow in confidence, the more that Gwen retreated. She was refusing to take part in any of the scenes for the showcase and was quieter and more remote than the girls had ever seen her.

Darrell was at her wits' end about the whole thing. Miss Grayling had specifically stated that every girl was to participate and Darrell knew that Gwen's parents and old governess were travelling a long way to see her perform. Much as she sometimes found it hard to like Gwendoline, Darrell had a kind heart and she couldn't bear to think of Gwen's humiliation at being the only person not involved in the showcase, especially when she had done her best to make amends with Maggie.

The next few hours were a whirlwind of activity. There were costumes to adjust and props to find and last-minute nerves to settle. Darrell and Sally raced from one place to the next, ensuring that everything was ready. And then it was time.

Darrell stood on the stage and peeped out from behind the curtain as the audience assembled.

'There's Mother and Father!' she whispered to Sally. 'And I can see your parents too! And, oh, there's my younger sister, Felicity, and little Daphne!'

Sally peeped over Darrell's shoulder to get a glimpse of her little sister. 'There are so many people!' she murmured. 'Am I really to introduce everyone, Darrell?'

Darrell grinned and let the curtain drop. 'Yes, you are!' she told her. 'You've worked incredibly hard to organise us all and it should absolutely be you who welcomes all of our parents. Be brave, Sally – you can do this!'

And then she gave Sally a little push, propelling her through the curtains.

'Thank you for coming to North Tower Lower Fourth Showcase,' began Sally, her voice faltering on the first few words. 'I am very proud to present to you our very own Malory Towers art exhibition!'

She swept back her hand and the curtains swung open, revealing Belinda. She was perched on a stool and sitting very still, wearing a painter's smock and holding a brush in her hand. The easel in front of her held a half-finished piece of work but what caught the audience's attention was the art displayed around the stage. It included some of Belinda's finest work, with a few pieces from other girls who were also skilled artists.

'That's really very good,' muttered one mother to another. 'Some of these paintings wouldn't look out of place in a London gallery.'

Behind the curtain Darrell swelled with pride for her friend.

Sally gave them time to look at everything and then, after a few minutes, signalled to Irene who started playing on the piano that stood at the side of the auditorium. The curtains swooshed closed and the girls rushed on to the stage to remove the easels and set up for the next scene, which involved a swathe of deep blue shimmery material held up by Mavis and Mary-Lou while Alicia perched on top of a ladder in her bathing costume, poised as if she was about to dive into the water.

'It all looks incredible,' whispered Maggie, coming up behind Darrell and peeking out. 'Oh – I can see my mother in the audience! I wasn't sure if she would be able to come! Aunt and Uncle Lacey must have brought her. That was good of them – it's just a shame that their daughter isn't capable of the same kindness.'

Darrell made a decision. Turning to Maggie, she pulled the other girl away from the edge of the stage and into the wings.

'You do know that it was only because Gwen went looking for you that you were rescued that day on the sand spit, don't you?' she said quietly. 'She came to find you to say sorry for being so beastly.'

Maggie frowned. 'So why hasn't she said anything to me?' she asked. 'She hasn't even *tried* to apologise for being so unwelcoming.'

Darrell looked Maggie right in the eye. 'She has been

trying,' she told her. 'But you haven't exactly been letting her, have you?'

Maggie flushed and looked down at the floor. Darrell heard applause from the auditorium and, peering over Maggie's shoulder, saw that the curtain had risen on Alicia's daring diving scene.

'Besides,' she said, turning her focus back to Maggie, 'there are lots of ways to say sorry. Gwen might not have said it with words but she's been trying to show you with her actions. Where do you think your new dance pumps came from?'

Maggie's eyes darted to her feet. 'Are you telling me that *she* gave these to me?' she asked faintly. 'My cousin, Gwendoline Mary?'

'The very same,' Darrell assured her. 'She's desperate to make it better but she doesn't know how to tell you.'

The curtains swished shut again and Darrell stepped forward.

'I've got to go and pose for the lacrosse scene now,' she said. 'You need to be ready for the dance scene at the very end, OK?'

Maggie nodded and walked off, looking dazed.

Darrell rushed on to the stage where some of the other girls were already waiting, frozen in position with their lacrosse sticks held in mid-air, ready for Darrell to join their midst and arrange herself so that it looked like she was about to score a goal.

The rest of the showcase went exactly as planned. The girls posed in a scene from the French classroom with Sally dressed as Mam'zelle Dupont, wearing a frightful wig that someone had discovered in the drama cupboard. They showed the stables with Bill tending to her horse, or rather a magnificent cardboard cut-out of Thunder that Belinda had created, the real animal having been banned from the stage by Miss Grayling, much to Bill's disgust.

And then it was time for the grand finale. The curtains closed and the girls rushed to move the stable props. Mavis dimmed the lights and Maggie walked slowly on to the middle of the stage. The lower fourth gathered themselves in the wings, grinning at each other in excitement. It had all been a complete success and the only thing left to do now was to let Maggie's dancing end the show.

Irene raised her hands, waiting for her cue to conduct the school orchestra who had spent hours rehearsing her own composition, created specially for Maggie and this moment. But then Maggie paused before turning and walking back towards where the girls were standing.

'When I first got here I didn't want to be a Malory Towers girl,' she said, her gaze focused on one person in particular. Her voice was quiet and there was no way that the audience could hear her, but the girls in the wings could hear every word.

'What's she doing?' Sally asked Darrell. 'We've almost finished and it's gone so well – I can't bear for it to be ruined now.'

'Just wait,' whispered Darrell.

'I thought that you were all stuck up and I didn't think that you cared about anything except yourselves.' Maggie paused, looking at each one of them. 'But I was wrong and I *do* want to be a Malory Towers girl now, more than anything. When I first arrived Miss Grayling told me that Malory Towers girls should leave the school as women that the world can depend on. I know that I can depend on all of you and I want to be as strong and kind as you are.'

She smiled. 'So will you dance with me? Will you help me to be a proper Malory Towers girl?'

And then she reached out her hand towards Gwen.

'Is it a trap?' whispered Alicia, leaning in towards Darrell. 'Is she going to make Gwen look stupid because I for one wouldn't blame her if she did!'

Darrell shook her head. 'I don't think so,' she said uncertainly. 'But we all know that Gwen can't dance so I can't imagine how this is going to work.'

Maggie nodded at Alicia, who leant out from the side of the curtain and gave the cue. The beautiful sounds of Irene's composition floated through the hall and the curtains began to open.

'I can't watch,' whimpered Sally, putting her head in

her hands. 'It's going to be ridiculous and everyone is going to laugh.'

'Please dance with me, Gwen,' murmured Maggie, pulling her forward. 'Let's dance away from everything that has happened and towards a new beginning.'

Gwen glanced around, spotting her mother and father and Miss Winter in the audience. They were smiling encouragingly and next to them was Maggie's mother, her face lit up with a huge smile.

Gwen accepted Maggie's hand and started to walk, her legs shaking.

'I can't dance,' she muttered, feeling her cheeks flush.

'Who says so?' Maggie whispered back as they reached the centre of the stage.

Gwen grimaced. 'I do,' she admitted. 'I'm not good at physical activities. Not like you. And just about everyone thinks that I'm lazy and useless.'

'But it doesn't matter what they think,' said Maggie, picking up both Gwen's hands and holding them in her own. 'It matters what *you* think.'

A spotlight came on and the two girls froze in position, lit up from above. And then, ever so slowly, Maggie started to dance, moving in time to Irene's melodic tune. Small steps to begin with and then, as Gwen gained confidence, larger movements until the two girls were dancing together on the stage hand in hand. When the music finally came to end the audience rose to their feet. And nobody was cheering louder than the lower fourth, who raced on to the stage and surrounded the two girls.

'Well done, Maggie! Well done, Gwen!' called Sally.

'Bravo!' shouted Darrell, clapping so hard that her hands started to sting.

'That was wonderful!' Alicia emitted one of her dreadful ear-piercing whistles, which caused Mam'zelle, who was sitting close to the stage, to fling her hands over her ears in fright. 'Who knew that you could dance like that, Gwen? You dark horse!'

'It wasn't me,' said Gwen, collapsing on to the stage next to her cousin as the applause died down and the parents started to chat among themselves. 'It was Maggie.'

'It was both of you,' said Darrell, grinning at Sally. 'What a wonderful way to end the show!'

'That was brilliant,' sighed Sally contentedly, sitting down on the stage floor as Irene and the others came to join them. 'I really think we showed everyone the very best things about North Tower and the lower fourth.'

'I can't wait for next term,' said Maggie, taking off her dance pumps and wriggling her toes. 'Miss Potts said that I can organise a Christmas extravaganza and I'm going to make sure that every single one of you is involved in the dancing, so get practising over the summer holidays!'

'Maybe you could come and practise with me sometime?' ventured Gwen, her voice sounding unusually shy. 'I could ask Mother and Father if you could stay with us.'

Maggie cast a glance over to where everyone was chatting. She could see her mother talking enthusiastically to Gwen's parents and smiling with delight at something that Mrs Lacey had said. She thought about how filled with despair she had been when her aunt and uncle had insisted on sending her away to school and how, in the end, it had all worked out for the best.

'Or perhaps you could come and stay with us?' she suggested, a mischievous look on her face. 'You know, if you don't mind living like a poor church mouse for a week?'

Gwen flushed. 'I would love to visit your home.'

Maggie clasped her hand and grinned. 'It'll be bread and soup for every meal, I'm warning you!'

'I will enjoy every mouthful,' said Gwen bravely, although she looked so worried about the prospect that Maggie burst into peals of laughter that soon spread around the whole group.

'Here's to a fabulous showcase!' spluttered Darrell, gasping for breath. 'And a wonderful summer filled with fun!'

Enid Blyton

MALORY TOWERS

Read them all!

ENIDBLYTON.CO.UK

IS FOR PARENTS, CHILDREN AND TEACHERS!

Sign up to the newsletter on the homepage for a monthly round-up of news from the world of

Enid Blyton®

JOIN US ON SOCIAL MEDIA

EnidBlytonOfficial  BlytonOfficial

Enid Blyton®

is one of the most popular children's authors of all time. Her books have sold over 500 million copies and have been translated into other languages more often than any other children's author.

Enid Blyton adored writing for children. She wrote over 600 books and hundreds of short stories. *The Famous Five* books, now 75 years old, are her most popular. She is also the author of other favourites including *The Secret Seven*, *The Magic Faraway Tree*, *Malory Towers* and *Noddy*.

Born in London in 1897, Enid lived much of her life in Buckinghamshire and adored dogs, gardening and the countryside. She was very knowledgeable about trees, flowers, birds and animals. Dorset – where some of the Famous Five's adventures are set – was a favourite place of hers too.

Enid Blyton's stories are read and loved by millions of children (and grown-ups) all over the world. Visit enidblyton.co.uk to discover more.